THE NE
a fable o

C000055193

Michael Russell

First published in 2007 by
Balnakeil Press, 2 Balnakeil, Durness, Sutherland,
IV27 4PT, Scotland.
Telephone: (44) – 01971-511777
Email: lochcroispol@btopenworld.com
Website: www.balnakeilpress.com
www.scottish-books.net

ISBN: 978-1-905974-00-9

British Library Cataloguing-in-Publication Data
A catalogue record for this book is available from the British Library

Printed and bound by Cox & Wyman Ltd, Reading, Berkshire.

Michael Russell was brought up in Ayrshire and educated there and in Edinburgh. He has lived and worked in the Western Isles, Inverness-shire and Lanarkshire but for the past 14 years has been resident in rural Argyll. He is a well-known Scottish writer and commentator who contributes regularly to television, radio and the press. A front-bench member of the Scottish Parliament from 1999 to 2003, he is the author, co-author or editor of a number of non-fiction books. *The Next Big Thing* is his first novel.

By the same author:

Glasgow 1990: The Book (Editor)

Edinburgh: A Celebration (Editor)

A Poem of Remote Lives: the enigma of Werner Kissling

In Waiting: travels in the shadow of Edwin Muir

A Different Country

Stop the World: the autobiography of Winnie Ewing (Editor)

Grasping the Thistle
(with Dennis MacLeod)

… every country is prood of da wye at hit speaks
An sae we sood be prood o wirs to.

Rhoda Bulter, "Shetlandic"

There are places I'll remember
All my life, though some have changed
Some forever, not for better
Some have gone and some remain

John Lennon, "In My Life"

1. WHATEVER GETS YOU THRU THE NIGHT

Donald, his hair stirred by the wind and all of his six feet two inches leaning sideways, veered leftwards to avoid a pile of dog shit on the pavement deposited despite the local by-laws and regardless of the best attentions of the Scottish Parliament. He wondered if the next hour was going to bring both execution and blessed release.

A malevolent seagull fixed him with an aiming stare, ready to avenge the missed booby trap of excrement on behalf of the right of all animals to perform their bodily functions to Donald's maximum inconvenience, but even a drenching in the stuff would not have distracted him from his sense of impending doom, though he had to admit that the feeling was accompanied by a faint tingle of relief. Might there be, at last, a way out of this life and this place

The problem lay in his enquiring mind. A mind that could not keep itself focused even for the necessary few moments it took to avoid minor if inconvenient pitfalls, but instead got distracted by ideas. And then worried those ideas to death.

What is, after all, a suitable subject for a lifetime's study, thought Donald Or that part of a lifetime in which we choose to or are driven to study

For people choose or have chosen for them many things: the verb in old Icelandic, sewage systems in Ancient Rome, minute divisions of parts of molecules, the cure for cancer, the use of the comma in the works of an unknown poet, the finding of weapons of mass destruction (or not), the possibility of cloning one's lost child or the reason why so many of us can't stop eating burgers. The list, like human curiosity, is endless and, also like human curiosity, sometimes touching, occasionally farcical and frequently unfathomable.

The wind tugged at Donald's grubby jacket as he came round the corner of an ugly and ill-designed building, and one moreover thoroughly ill-suited for the margins of a Scottish seaside town. Half tower block, half toilet block, its white tiles had been streaked with grey within a month of its opening and were now pitted by salt and sand scour. Its micro-climate was vicious, producing on the calmest day – and this was not the calmest day – gusts which blew even the warily familiar university staff across the badly fitting paving stones towards scrubby flower-beds and strips of threadbare lawn.

As ever, the sight of the fitfully beating heart of the institution in which he served stirred up in Donald a nostalgia for the city of his birth, which lay only fifty miles to the south. He had grown up in a suburb of Edinburgh, and from a young age he had spent his time wandering that city, up and down the High Street, in and out of the closes, across the wide divide that separated Old Town and New, and even as far as the dirty, unkempt shores of the Forth on which the place had until recently turned its back.

He got to know that mad god's dream. He got to know how strange it was, all fur coat and nae knickers, full of places of wealth alongside places of poverty, its people addicted to what they thought were the dismal dichotomies of the Scottish character (Burke and Hare, Jekyll and Hyde) though they are utterly normal in every human being. It was a city obsequiously ceremonial, piously grand, sensual but in hiding, romantic and beautiful, in waiting for a role it gave away and every inch of it (as in the whole country

8

which it served yet lorded over) could yield up a thousand stories, except that most of its inhabitants were too busy and self-centred to ask what they were and – as a result – perilously few people know anything of them.

That neglect by his own parents, keenly making their way in a world in which they wanted Donald to keep rising, was perhaps what made Donald do it – to show, in fits and starts and with an eventual obsessiveness that made his teachers ask if he might be dyslexic, a passion not for going forward but for looking back. For finding out how things were, so that he could understand how they are now, and what they might be.

How they might be – how they had ended up – was a problem, it seemed to Donald. Back then it was 1970s Scotland, a very different Scotland from today's, the time of the three-day week, the city plunged district by district into blackness, as distant Tory governments asked in panic who governed Britain and got the answer – not them (though they would be back). Yet it was also the moment when the national psyche stirred, its confidence lubricated by oil and an unexpected second chance even if that did once more lead to self-inflicted disappointment.

Then it was 1980s Scotland, a hunched-shouldered, "here's tae us, wha's like us" decade when we comforted ourselves with the fact that we were too wise to be bothered with matters as intangible as our country and our duty towards it and when we looked enviously at those whose goal was making money. A time in which any of your neighbours or friends might find themselves not rich, but suddenly unemployed and very poor, yet a time in which the fear of poverty and loss inspired not collective solidarity, but individual greed.

But nothing lasts for ever and in the 1990s we were beginning to wonder if we could after all get things right – because those down south were getting them dreadfully

9

wrong. By that decade Donald was through school and almost through university (though his university was in another city, colder and drearier far than Edinburgh). His interest was in what was around him, and with the help of those few people who were interested too – the old city guides, a couple of teachers, the writers of the books that he guzzled down – he had begun to seriously study history as the key to where we were and where we might be going. Scottish history, of course, but it was a discipline that was not available everywhere.

Donald, of course, was not unique. He had been like most adolescents, not least because he thought himself unique. Pimply, lonely, manic, guilty and furtive, he mixed all of his selves together, plummeting from doubt to anger and swooping sometimes up insane happiness. But hopeful at times too, and dreaming at times, and thus able to hear what the world was whispering.

In those eighties and nineties university was a place to try and get a qualification on which to base a career, a simple equation which unfortunately negated the real purpose of education.

Fortunately Donald saw the point of learning and voyaged off in exploration. He sailed through his ordinary classes, and then with a little more effort found himself beaming out of his graduation photographs, holding a first-class honours degree in Scottish history much to the bemusement and frustration of his parents who had hoped he might settle down and become something useful, like an accountant or even a lawyer. Particularly as his overdraft was burgeoning.

The mental shape of the word 'overdraft' almost brought him back to full consciousness. He was standing now, or rather huddling, in a dank little inshot between the university tower and the wall of an old house, a spot in which nicotine addicts like himself gathered so that they would not pollute the virtuous lungs of fellow citizens. This was another of the Scottish Parliament's diktats, but Donald now liked the sense of guilt it produced so much that he enjoyed smoking more than he ever had before.

He looked at his watch, and realised that he was already late; the summons he had received fifteen minutes earlier had said "now" and the one who summonsed had an uncanny sense of how long it took to get from anywhere to his august and decisive presence. He dropped the cigarette in a sand-filled metal container, and reached to light another. The condemned man and all that, he thought, as the flame from his plastic lighter nipped his stained fingers.

He had started smoking when he left university as part of his re-definition: his remaking of his image post academia. In his department they had wanted him to stay on and complete a doctorate, and then enter the fray teaching a discipline that was hard to justify in terms of imparting earning power, or producing product ideas for exploitation. But Donald wanted a change, and a chance to find out more about his country which seemed to be, in Shakespeare's words, "Almost afraid to know itself". So he applied for every job he could find that was nowhere near either Edinburgh or his university town, and – somewhat quicker than he expected – was soon ensconced in a tourist office on a Hebridean island, managing a small staff of mostly local girls and older women, who worked seasonally to service the enquiries of those daring or foolish enough to venture off the beaten track.

Most people stay in such jobs for a year or so, before moving on. Donald, however, settled down, tried to learn Gaelic (a few people still spoke it where he was, though their natural insecurity about it meant that it took time and trust before they would speak it to anyone who wanted to learn) and started to study for his part-time PhD. His subject was all around him: it was the ignorance of his fellow

11

countrymen and -women about their own past, about their land and people, and what they could learn from it to make them move forward.

In contrast those from other places, furth of Scotland, who visited his little office (though there were progressively fewer as the years went on) seemed fired with enthusiasm. They would ask questions, seek information, and consume the few flimsy publications that Donald had encouraged local people to make available. Of course Donald contributed to that small trickle-down of learning as well.

It took some time to find a university that would accept his offbeat idea for intensive study, particularly intensive study from a great distance. It took even more time for Donald to complete it, because he had found that the island way of life suited him perfectly. He would be busy (or sort of busy) from May to September. He would be almost completely idle from September to May, with just about enough work to occupy an hour or so a day if he tried to make it last. Yet he would not spend that time reading and writing, as he should have. He would fish, he would walk, he would listen to music, and he would spend long hours just thinking – an occupation much under-rated in our world.

Oh, and he would have affairs. They were usually with local girls who had come home to teach, or incoming girls who had come away from home to teach. Donald worked his way through both the primary schools on the island and the neighbouring secondary school (with diversions for other professions, of course, particularly barmaids) but such was his diffident charm and his extraordinary detached but yet intense conversation that he did so without breaking many hearts, or causing much rivalry. In his affairs, as in his life, he was laid-back to almost a dangerous extreme. He was, in the words of P. G. Wodehouse, a man born one drink below par.

And of course he drank. Steadily, in company and out of company, and sometimes in binges. It was the island way and it suited him.

But there was one affair that was different. In what turned out to be his second last summer on the island, when his thesis was winding its way to completion, one of the new temporary staff from the mainland brought an excitement to the office that Donald had not experienced before. Susan was bright, companionable and attractive. She was quick of mind and she had a sentimental streak which suited the place and the people. It also suited Donald and before long they were sharing nights in the bar, and nights by the loch, and then nights all night in Donald's croft house down by the pier.

Donald paused again in reflection. He dropped the second cigarette, and beating against the wind which was stirring up old fag packets and bits of Styrofoam coffee containers, he made his way to the stiff glass doors beyond which stood the lifts which asthmatically wheeze him up to the inner sanctum.

He glimpsed a girl across the lift lobby, and momentarily felt the uplift of scared anticipation, for it could be Susan, though of course it couldn't be.

In any case Susan couldn't last and she didn't. The nights turned into days of debate and conversation about their future (beware of relationships which consist mostly of talking about the future – it usually means there isn't one). Susan had a degree to finish, and the city to return to. She asked him to come back and join her, but he wouldn't because he had a thesis to finish and a lifestyle to settle back into. The debates, and the summer, wound their way to autumn and the end. Susan left, and Donald missed her – endlessly. She wrote and e-mailed endlessly. And then slowly the messages became shorter and less frequent. Donald flirted with a new teacher. Susan decided that it was over. Donald concurred, and then it hurt more. It was soon winter. But it was a different winter, for Donald had started to think about his future again. Women can have that effect on men, especially able, confident and intelligent women when they meet able, confident and intelligent men who are standing just off-centre to the universe.

Thus it was that just nine months later Donald finished his thesis. It caused something of a stir, not least amongst the academic staff who had got used to his distant non-presence. And it stirred Donald too. For the first time in years he felt there might be other places he needed to see and other things he needed to do, but he had done nothing about doing them when an extraordinary offer came. Would he present himself for interview at the University of Seafield, where a new position in a new department might suit him well

He did. He found that the mainstream of Scotland had changed since he went away. Now history and tourism and how they are connected was all in vogue. Careers were being made, books were being written (his thesis was published as a book, much to his astonishment) and Scotland was once again a suitable subject for study. He was asked to fill the new position. So he did.

The lift doors opened and he entered like a man going to his final hour. He had even felt that fear the first time he had stood here, realising before Professor Lochhead had even grasped his hand in some sort of secret faculty grip that he was making a fearful mistake. He knew he would not be nearly as happy as he had been in his little office overlooking the pier, or in his little house by the pier. He was hemmed in by timetables, performance grids, strategic thinking and commercial sponsorship. He lived in dread of supervision, assessment, attainment targets and academic league tables. Just as he had known that his time in the islands was drawing to a close, soon he knew that his time at the University of Seafield was not unlimited. He and his department were an accident waiting to happen.

It was happening now. He was disgorged on a floor that might have come out of another building – a better-designed, richer, more civilised building than this could be or ever had been. Dark blue carpets, small bright pictures on the wall, up-lighting that emphasised space all surrounded by an ozone-rich atmosphere of calm but busy efficiency. He glanced at the protector of the place, hoping he would have to wait, but she simply waved him through, though with a look of contempt that brought back to mind the dog shit he had only recently avoided.

The corridor was designed to intensify the feeling of over-confidence and awe. The pictures were bigger, the lighting darker, and the door at the end gleamed maliciously. He paused before knocking, an image of Susan coming into his mind unbidden.

He thought he almost understood her now. She too, after all, had had her disappointments. To her, Donald was infuriating, charming, entertaining, exciting, knowledgeable, lacking in ambition, and (above all) everything she was looking for, including the things she didn't know she was looking for. Except that she felt she should not be looking, that there was more out there, and that to find so much so easily was somehow wrong. It might just lead to another let-down. And she wanted above everything to find herself and know herself, not just be found by, and be known for, someone else.

So she finished her degree and decided to get away. As the islands were out of the equation (too many memories, too many chances of seeing Donald) she sought out the first job she could find that was far away and which she could also do far too easily. Soon she too was sitting in a little office by a pier (though that pier was attached to the northern mainland), managing the girls and the women who worked in the season when there might be work to do. Imitation is the sincerest form of flattery although she would have denied any such thing vigorously.

He knocked and waited. Somewhere in his mind was a fact that he was grasping for. It was, unfortunately, nothing to do with what he would have to say in here, nor the questions he would have to answer, couched in language he could barely understand.

The fact was that none of this would be happening if he had ever been fired with the ambition to achieve. Nor would it have happened had Susan decided to work abroad that summer, or if the two of them had listened to what their hearts were telling them in those long and beautiful nights on the island, closely lying in the box bed in the old croft house.

It had been two years since Donald went to Seafield. About the same time had elapsed since Susan went north. And now, he knew, it was all about to change again. "Come," said a voice from the other side of the impossibly shiny door.

2. NOWHERE MAN

The University of Seafield was not in the first rank of Scottish universities, but the ambitions of its Vice Chancellor, Principal, Chief Executive and Guiding Spirit were fortunately not directed towards gaining the patina of age and refined respectability. To be in the public eye was the ambition of the institution and of its Head, and the two ambitions blended happily into constant exposure even if one part of the marriage predominated.

Professor Lochhead craved nothing but the reputation for modernity. If academic relevance was a craze, then he was the spinning dervish at the heart of it, constantly on the whirring lookout for new disciplines, new subjects to have endowed, and new financing which could stick to anything it chose. He rejoiced in the wounds inflicted by the cutting edge.

Yet today, standing with his back to his desk, staring out onto the Scottish seascape that dominated every view from his university, he was a troubled man and the wounds were stinging – or at least one wound.

It was true that for the University of Seafield no electronics were micro enough, no form of media too transitory, no passing dietary fad too outlandish to evade what passed for academic consideration.

Whilst some might have baulked at embracing line dancing as a suitable subject for study, Professor Lochhead was quickly dazzled by the potential media interest, and the opportunity for one of his people (they were always "his" people until his interest waned) to be heard commenting learnedly at the world championship. Curriculum sponsorship from a leather tassel manufacturer in deepest Arizona followed. For a while Seafield echoed to the sound of Hank, Hoss and the Honkey Tonks (though the Vice Chancellor was a Grace Williams fan).

Chairs of Aerobics and Cartoon Studies had been established within months of his arrival at Seafield. But Professor Lochhead was a restless man, as his acquisition of three wives (all ex-students) tended to show.

Five years on he was in his second phase (and nearly fourth wife), weeding out the courses he already regarded as past their prime, despite having championed them what seemed only weeks before (the social scientists had got mired in the world of Tamagochis, much to their subsequent regret).

"Change, modernise, be relevant," he would tell his board of managers, most of whom recognised in the mantra simply a need for more diverting, blue sky plans in their weekly reports, publication schedules and course outlines, which already veered close enough to being works of fiction to qualify them for examination as part of "Shagging, Drinking and Scribbling", Seafield's approach to the study of the Scottish creative impulse.

"Change, modernise, be relevant," he muttered, watching the long waves crash into the dirty beach just below his window.

Unfortunately it was a mantra that was causing difficulty for his Department of Applied Tourism.

In his heady prime, he had seen Applied Tourism as being at the apogee of his plans. What was more relevant to the faded seaside town beside which the once white towers of the university now rose like a form of grey speckled fungus At the height of summer, a tourist boom for the town would provide useful extra income for the university, providing the student cells could be tarted up a little. But the town would need a make-over, and something to make it worth visiting. Applied Tourism could apply itself to the town first, while drawing in endless students for short courses in the winter, all keen to know how to squeeze more and more profit from their MacHaggis restaurant, or their "Bide-a-wee" craft shop. And what would brighten the place up more on dull days like this than the sight and sound and perhaps even touch of such eager and willing-to-learn goddesses of the tourist trade as the golden-haired manageress of a bakery in Hawick that he had once glimpsed over the sausage rolls

Persuading a donor to sponsor the department proved easier than he had imagined. An American soft drinks company was looking to buy market share, so the Hi-Fizz Department of Applied Tourism at the University of Seafield came into being, with the blessing of the passing minister at the Scottish Executive who was told that tourism was amongst his responsibilities if not his interests, and for whom association with commerce was an exciting novelty and a further brownie point in his remorseless rise in New Labour.

The Scottish Visitors Administration, the industry's statutory guide, watchdog and regulator but not friend had not been so sure. When government knew the cost of everything and the value of very little (and certainly not the inestimable value of a quiet life in a comfortable office block in a better part of Edinburgh, to which the Executive Director and Chairman of the SVA could comfortably commute in their chauffeur-driven Jaguars, at the tax payer's and the industry's expense) the Administration knew that discretion was the better part of valour. So more than ever the watchword was to say nothing, but always to seek the philosopher's stone that might turn tourist clichés into marketing catchphrases. Part of that process required

19

academic input and part required new sources of money, such as American drinks manufacturers so by means of civil servant to civil servant negotiations it managed to insinuate itself into the position of "external monitor" of the Hi-Fizz Department, much to Lochhead's resentment.

Putting that interference aside, all that Lochhead then had to do was to find the "right man" to make it all happen. Not that Lochhead was averse to finding the "right woman" should the need arise, and when the staffing statistics of Seafield began to look a trifle old-fashioned. But getting the "right" anything for the Department had proved the most difficult part of the process.

At first he had told his "scouts" (he liked the term, particularly as he thought of himself as some form of sporting manager, the Alex Ferguson of the academic world) to look amongst those already administering tourism. But that had not been a success.

The reports were deeply depressing. Nobody under 50, lots of problems with drink, tills (hands in them) and/or simple life-sapping, mind-numbing inertia. Plenty of interest, but nobody worth having.

He cast the net wider, scouting tourism entrepreneurs, hotel owners, even tour guides. Still nothing that would gild the towers of Seafield with ambition, drive and a healthy respect for his vision of academia. And then one morning he was brought a name. Donald Keays.

Keays had been overlooked in the original trawl because his background, and indeed present actions, were so unusual. Aged 30, he had been running a tourist office on the end of a Western Isles pier, observing at first hand the tourist market and tourists themselves, as part of his research for a doctoral thesis on the reactions of incoming visitors to the culture and history of Scotland, contrasted with that of Scottish people themselves. The thesis had been a long time in the researching, the combination of reluctance by any recognised history department in any recognised university to have anything to do with it, and Donald's own offbeat way of proceeding through life – a progress of fits and starts, with progressively less energetic starts and more and more rather idle fits.

But the thesis was finished and published and Dr Keays had made a small splash in some of the tabloid newspapers with the assertion that most visitors actually liked Scottish culture and history, the main impediment to their understanding and enjoyment being the fact that most Scots knew nothing about such subjects and cared even less.

"Doc says Scots are thick," said the *Daily Record*, in a piece which had not been burdened by the journalist having either read the thesis or talked to Donald. This had not worried the journalist, but it did worry Donald that evening in a Glasgow pub, where the grainy *Record* photograph had been enough to have him recognised, head-butted and then barred.

Lochhead always liked celebrities, particularly those whose 15 seconds of fame presented no threat of his own lustre being eclipsed. So Donald Keays, freshly capped and with a publication, found himself offered, and for the want of any other enticement accepting, the sole academic position in the Department of Applied Tourism, Seafield University.

Some two years later it was still the sole academic position, hovering between a Lecturer, a Researcher, and just someone who was there to take the blame. A part-time typist sent out his course information, organised the trickle of students and deflected all but the harshest enquiries from Lochhead's office. The study of how to make the town of Seafield the tourist mecca of the north, the production of which he had been urged to start immediately on appointment ("Change, modernise, be relevant," said Lochhead, *inter alia*) staggered on, most of it now conducted

21

by means of interview over the bar of the Ship Inn where Donald had established his most regular departmental base camp.

It was from there that he had been summoned by Professor Lochhead, his typist's holiday having removed the usual line of defence, and a stray student having reported to Lochhead's latest inamorata that she had heard that someone had once attended a tutorial there, sitting if not at Keays's feet, at least on the next bar stool.

The Vice Chancellor was aware of a noise. It was Donald clearing his throat. Donald was operating on a simple principle: take the bollocking and return to the Ship, where a pint still sat half-drunk on the bar. Even if it was to be his last.

Lochhead remained where he was, studying the waves. On his desk was the latest letter, in a long line, from Hi-Fizz wondering what was happening to their money but with a new edge as it looked at what was meant to be the new Scotland with hungry profit-centred eyes. Now it seemed that money might not continue to bubble from its eternal well. Profile, prestige and cash were at stake. And something more, as the headed notepaper of the Scottish Visitors Administration peeping out from the file ominously suggested.

Keays coughed again, and Lochhead turned his head to look at him.

"Donald."

First names were de rigueur with Lochhead, he rejoicing in being called "Peter" by everyone from the minor royal who was Chancellor (whom he called "Sir") to the disaffected cleaner who polished his desk twice a day and casually loathed him as she casually loathed everything about the university.

"Peter   "

22

"Donald." A long pause for effect. "Time is running out."

Donald was momentarily thrown by this gnomic remark. He hoped for a second it meant that the Vice Chancellor had another appointment, and he was in the process of levering himself to his feet when Lochhead turned to face him, and stepped into the lee of his desk.

"Something will have to be done with your department. Something perhaps like work, or students or even research. Where has your research progressed in this," his hands swept around, indicating Donald's entire kingdom, "benighted town "

"What," his voice rose to a crescendo, the volume seemingly lifting his eyebrows into an explosive arch, "exactly have you been doing "

Lochhead's eyebrows were amongst his finest features. He had them trimmed each time his leonine head of hair was burnished and shaped. The raising of his eyebrows to his staff was a gesture much mimicked in late-night parties across the faculties. But mimicry often has its roots in fear. Donald felt the fear.

"Well," he started. "Well, Peter. Well, Peter, it's been kind of hard."

Why kind of hard , he wondered, as he searched for the words that would get him out of here as quickly as possible Kind of hard because he was sick of tourism, or at least the way that it was seen by the pimple-faced students who thought they glimpsed an easy option in the dazzling array of strange courses that lay open to them, on a field not so much open to their talents as pockmarked with the cowpats of exams, assessment and failure.

Kind of hard because the Hi-Fizz sponsorship left his office long on soft drinks, but short on anything approaching guidance, support, or even genuine interest.

Kind of hard because he was tired of this town and the four walls of his dingy Victorian seaside flat and his dingy new brutalist seaside office and he missed – so much – the freedom of the island And missed the freedom of being with Susan too.

Or even kind of hard because he knew that the Vice Chancellor's enthusiasm had waned and that Donald had not the slightest interest, except self-preservation and the monthly injection of cash into his ballooning overdraft, in rekindling it. And even those motivations were fast ebbing in the harsh light of the reality of the job.

"What do you mean, 'Kind of hard' " barked the Vice Chancellor, cutting in on the multiple-choice answer that Donald was pondering. "Is it not 'kind of hard' for me to justify the sponsorship money month after month when nothing seems to be happening " "Is it not 'kind of hard' for me to defend you against a government body that has heard virtually nothing from you – and certainly nothing of interest – in two years, despite their support and encouragement "

"Well," started Donald again, conscious that this conversation was not presently even registering his presence.

"No wells about it, Donald," said the Vice Chancellor. "Something will have to be done. And fortunately I know what."

It was often said of the Vice Chancellor that he had survived for so long, and in so distinguished a fashion, because he had one skill that constantly got him out of trouble. It was the skill of invention, of taking a sudden sharp and unexpected track in meetings and conversations that always left his adversaries working out, usually too slowly, how to cut him off.

The Vice Chancellor, in a long low swoop past his desk, transferred himself from the window to the edge of

24

the table beside Donald. The parabola allowed him to grab a file from his blotter, and opening it, he brandished a letter in Donald's face.

Donald glimpsed the blocked logo of the SVA before the Vice Chancellor drew it back and started reading it in his lecturer's voice.

"As part of our five year target setting plan, and in connection with the current ongoing review of non departmental bodies, the Scottish Visitors Administration has been concerned to achieve both best value from the research and development project presently established by commercial sponsorship in your university and to identify potential growth points in the incoming visitors priority spend intentions. 'Hi-Fizz' has, as you know, recently entered into take over talks with 'Heather Pure' soft drinks of Lanarkshire, Scotland's fastest growing consumer drinks manufacturer and are keen to involve Heather Pure in tourist development. Several projects from different sources have presented themselves and accordingly 'Hi-Fizz' in its role as sponsor of the department, and ourselves as external monitor wish to review present funding arrangements and progress with the Seafield Tourism Development Project. I would be grateful therefore if you could arrange a meeting between your departmental staff, yourself, the Administration and Heather Pure at an early date in order to assess future options."

"Signed," said the Vice Chancellor, "by that oaf Charlie MacKellar, a placeman if ever I met one, but as he is placed both in the House of Lords and in the Chair of the benighted Visitor Administration not one we can afford to ignore."

"Departmental staff," said Donald, wondering anew if there was something about his department that only he failed to understand.

"That's you," said the Vice Chancellor. "Oh, and me in my capacity as titular Head of Department, a detail in the financing that need not concern you."

"Donald, this is important. It is fair to say that so far your department," – Your department really, Vice Chancellor, thought Donald, though recognising it was a thought best kept to himself – "has so far been a disappointment. 'Hi-Fizz' has not been pleased, the University Board has not been pleased, I have not been pleased."

Lochhead paused. He wanted the full impact of the implied threat to sink in before he produced his rabbit from its hat.

"You will recognise that the purpose of this letter is undoubtedly to allow the Visitor Administration, Hi-Fizz and who knows who else in to find out for themselves that we cannot – you cannot – run a piss-up in a brewery. And therefore go somewhere else, which is as we speak preparing to receive them. But," and he looked at Donald with eyebrows rising again, "that will not happen. And it will not happen because I have a plan."

Connoisseurs of Lochhead's style were familiar with this moment. It was the cusp on which many futures had depended, not least Lochhead's own from time to time. "The plan" usually came to nothing in the end, but the new momentum swept all problems before it for long enough to save those up to their neck in whatever it was.

"Plan   "

"Yes, plan. 'Hi-Fizz' are looking for something else. Hi-Fizz want to be a force in Scottish tourism, they want profit and they want it through 'Heather Pure', because 'Heather Pure' has been looking for something new in tourism for months. They haven't found it," – and here the Vice Chancellor leant forward so that Donald's eyes met his own – "but you will!"

26

"You will!" he repeated for theatrical emphasis (he being his own best and most appreciative audience). "You will find the next big thing in tourism, engage the interest of Heather Pure, Hi-Fizz and the Visitor Administration and save yourself and your department."

("And you," thought Donald, again silently.)

Lochhead paused and glanced back at the window, where the sea and sky were swapping shades of darkening grey either because a storm was building up (it has built up already in here, thought Donald) or because it was Scotland.

"I have asked Alice [the Vice Chancellor's long-suffering secretary] to set the meeting. About three weeks hence should do. By then I want a work plan and some ideas. I have already set the wheels in motion to produce a new budget, which of course will reflect the increased costs we will incur. Ask the finance department for the parts that concern you, especially travel.

"When we meet them we are going to tell them that our Seafield project is dead. Dead because we have been doing something much more exciting. We are going to sell them a new project, and one that will give them the newest, the biggest and the best attraction they can imagine. Something they can name and own and which I have brought them. Something that needs years – years, Donald – of nurturing and research.

"You are going to sell them that vision. Or rather I am, and you are going to be grateful enough to do the work so that I can."

Donald by now had nothing to say. In a part of him there was a grudging but great admiration for the lifeline that the Vice Chancellor had manufactured from nowhere, in the space of a few minutes. But it was the type of admiration a victim might have for his mugger, an admiration for the speed of the cosh or the strength of the boot. Donald knew he could not find the next useless thing, still less the next big thing. Indeed it probably didn't exist. But how on earth could he say it, and keep not just a job, but also his credit rating

For a moment he almost did, just to get it all over with, but the moment had no chance to come. There was a beep from deep inside the Vice Chancellor's pocket, and his left hand dived straight in to retrieve a mobile phone. He grimaced, rattled out a text (the university's Department of Linguistics was big on academic examination of texting – Lochhead had seen to that) and then glanced at Donald.

"Next meeting, I'm afraid. Let me have your plan the day before the meeting. And get to it now, not back to that sleazy pub."

A minute or two later Donald found himself outside again, almost as if he had been teleported. A gale was rising, lifting what little earth there was from the borders and scouring the building once more. His head made for his office in the next block but one. His feet, however, were already moving back to the comfort of the snug bar at the Ship and his feet redirected his head within seconds.

The Ship was still empty, his pint still on the bar. But as he took his first sip he was conscious that it tasted different. There was a bitterness to it that he had not felt an hour (he looked at his watch – fifty-two minutes actually) before. It was as if all of him, including his taste buds, had changed in that brief almost-hour, and changed somewhat for the worse.

The steady drift of his life seemed suddenly to have stopped. Either the raft that wandered about for years with him reclining on it had sunk, or else it had been swept out into deep water, and towards a Corryvreckan.

He had always known that doing nothing and being paid for it was not going to last for ever, and indeed sometimes he wished that he would experience a

28

revolution, one in which someone found a role and purpose for his thirty-two-year-old existence.

It had to happen, but he had expected it would happen in a way that would make him feel new and energised and ready for the challenge. But this was simply a sentence of execution, a challenge too far. Where would he find the enthusiasm, or the ability, to chase the next big thing Where indeed was the next big thing in a country where small things were all that people expected, and perhaps all that they might be able to cope with

The Vice Chancellor was right. It was a set-up. He was being set up for the termination of his funding and his tenure. But the Vice Chancellor was wrong if he thought that all it took was one bound to be free. It was a set-up in which the trap would close, and in its jaws would be the Department of Applied Tourism and all it contained, which wasn't much but him.

Night did not so much fall on Seafield even in these spring-becoming-summer months, as settle with a heavy sigh. Someone switched the lights on in the bar and Donald stared out of the small glass window, which like every window in Seafield, gave a glimpse of the cold expanse of the North Sea. Very cold, even now.

The Vice Chancellor was right. Something needed to be done. Something must be done.

Donald called for another pint. He knew that it would be the second of many that evening.

3. MAGICAL MYSTERY TOUR

There are many Scotlands. Some exist only in heads, turning and tossing on pillows across five continents. Some exist in books, on screens, in conversations in bars, at the back of eyes turning to the wall for the last time: in every place and circumstance where there are human beings and the all-too-human need for hope or blame or explanation. A few are the stuff of speeches and political dreams. And then, of course, there are the real ones.

The real Scotlands peep up over hills and rises, suddenly emerge from mist and rain clouds, come into being as night folds itself away into dawn, assemble round street corners or sliver in silver as moonlight crosses water. Start off from any of Scotland's cities and you can discover a dozen such Scotlands in the course of a day's journey. But you are still not even halfway to where you might end up going.

Scotland is like a layer cake. The easy-to-get-to, nearly-not-ours sponge at the bottom is full of Borders sweetmeats – Jeddart snails, Hawick balls, Moffat toffees. They are like the hills themselves, soft and gooey on the outside, solid and heart-shattering as rock within. They are bound to hurt you if you grow too fond of them, and they will never truly be yours.

Then there is the chocolate. The cities, the industrial zones, the playground beaches of the old rivieras and the distant prospect of higher ground and cleaner air. You can gorge yourself on this Scotland and never leave it. You can believe it is the best there is and yet still find yourself on a summer day wondering about the firth or river or looking north to the snow-topped hills, and wondering what lies beyond, and why.

Above the chocolate is something firm – marzipan perhaps, shaped into incredible inclines, cloying and unreal. It

30

stretches for miles up one side, but hardly at all upon the other. It is the horns on which Scotland's dilemma sits – the icing, old and solid and with the odd sparkle of glitter still left from celebrations long done. It is the real Scotland, it believes, yet it is vast and desolate and no longer of great account to its more popular, more digestible confections in the south. Year by year it is losing its sweetness, losing its sugar, losing its very character. And yet it remains.

Bits, of course, have broken off. And at the very top, nearer to heaven or further from humanity, lies the distant edge of Scotland, the Scotland which is more uncluttered and more uncrowded than any other place you know.

Not that it is empty. In the summer the roads are busy bearing, amongst others, German cars with too-healthy-looking occupants playing Runrig tapes and proudly displaying "The Black Forest Welcomes Donnie" on their bumpers even though Donnie is no longer with Runrig and never visits the Black Forest. The sheep stare at them and they stare back.

All the mod cons you could want are available in this part of Scotland although they can only be had at a price. True, you might be able to find a filling station with a back-up hand-cranked pump in case the electricity fails, but usually the vastly expensive fuel (the profit sucked out by a Scottish Chancellor in exile who knows little about the heartlands of his home) flows unimpeded with an electric hum, and the clink of the digital cash register can be heard all the way down to the cave where the little boats ride at anchor attached to orange pompoms.

And you can see as they pass the Dormobiles from Dagenham or the caravans from Colchester, people touring with their homes on their back, keen to experience what they believe is their country until they get there, when they realise that it isn't.

When the sun shines in this place the landscape becomes alive with those who still live here, who treat the brightness and warmth as a signal to do the things that can only be done now: the cutting of peats, the gathering and shearing of sheep, the sitting outside on the doorstep and watching what is happening in their

31

world. *Watching the seagulls dive on the tiny fishing boats far out in the firth, or the coloured cagoules coming down the mountainside, each containing someone who has never seen this place before and, unlucky person, may never come to it again.*

In the sunshine it is magical here on the coast. But travel a couple of miles inland – take the road back to the south, though it is many hours before you can arrive at such a definition of where you are – and the magic becomes darker and less human. "Miles and miles of bugger-all," said the old woman who had lived there for sixty years of her life, and never wanted to at all. Miles and miles of bugger-all indeed, except the careful kindly eye can see the magnificence of the eagle on the wind, the tender deer frightened by the smell of hunting humans, the bemused rabbit hurtling to finish its short life, the cold efficient splash of a salmon returning upriver to its home and the breath-taking beauty of sharp grass bending with the wind.

Click the shutter. Take this view. Turn up the magnification and see the outlines of ruined houses on steep sides beside the loch. Zoom out and see what little sign there is of lived-in habitation across all the moor. People are not the focus of this landscape and perhaps never were. But there were more people a generation ago, and a generation before that. Their children and grandchildren are somewhere else. There are stories about each one of them, even though many of the stories appear to have died in a last telling under an alien sky. Ghosts here have no children yet always the words and the deepest memories remain.

Those stories are the children of this landscape. Someday a few of them will return home, albeit to an uncertain welcome.

4. ISOLATION

There were times when Susan didn't like her job. But they were only the times when she was forced to do it in the bureaucratic and distant way her employers wanted. Fortunately such times were mercifully rare, not least because her sense of duty was now overwhelmingly to those amongst whom she lived and to the place which she had come to love. She always put them, and her feelings for them, first.

This morning she felt that love more strongly than ever, as she walked on the long strand that stretched for miles from the old kirkyard, past the headland. But although there was no call for her to work today (the tourist season being so brief in these parts that even a fine May morning did not produce anything approaching a rush), she was worrying about work.

Or more specifically she was worrying about the potential for there being not just no work, but no money in return for work which, put bluntly, was, if not any longer her reason for being here, at least the one that made it possible.

Whilst for the Scottish Visitor Administration the idea of visitors was an abstract, a matter of statistics, market penetration, outward missions and inward delegations, for Susan tourism was a simple matter of numbers. Numbers of people who phoned or wrote during the winter and who, in what passed for summer in these parts, opened the door which rang the buzzer in her tourist centre or who could be counted on the returns from the handful of bed and breakfast outlets that still thought it worth reporting and did not bitterly grudge the subscription that required them to do so – a subscription that ensured only a range of intermittent and increasingly doubtful benefits.

When Susan had left university – in fact when Susan had gone to university – she had absolutely no idea what work she wanted to undertake. Whilst those around her were consumed with the necessity of getting on and getting up whatever ladder they had been pointed at, Susan simply lived her life, stepping over the obstacles put in her way whether they were low rocks or racing hurdles.

One of those obstacles was, she realised now, Donald Keays, who started off by being a low rock that she was prepared to dawdle over, intrigued (so to speak) by its lichen but who became in time the highest of hurdles. It was the existence of Donald Keays which, indirectly, had led to her being on this beach today. For one of her holiday jobs had taken her to a pier in the Western Isles and into the orbit of the manager of the tourist information centre who had, if not swept her off her feet, at least inveigled her into bed after several evenings of drink and laughter.

She had to admit that he was not handsome, nor even darkly ugly as so many attractive men were. He was just a little off-centre to life, with a way of seeing things that was infuriating, depressing but usually accurate. It was obvious, after all, that most people around them knew nothing about their country or its past but only Donald would spend the first part of his life proving it, and then the second failing to do anything about it.

But he was exciting and knowledgeable. He was entertaining and thoughtful. And in his company she felt more whole than she did with anyone else. In short she was happier with him than she had ever been with anyone else and he said that the same was true for him.

Yet she was not surprised that it had not lasted. Distance, the usual fears and her own doubts had sunk it over months, first of agonised conversation, and then of frantically pored over and deeply interpreted e-mails and letters. When it finally came to an end it had been easier (she knew) for him. Since then her heart had skipped a beat when mutual acquaintances gave some snippets of news or sightings although she always feigned disinterest, with a shrug of her shoulders and a dismissive wave of her hand.

For a while he had been stuck (at his own volition) in the same place but – surprisingly – he had then suddenly emerged in some sort of respectable, academic job in a hole of a place on the east coast of Scotland. By then she had taken the first job – one that would take her far away from his university and from any chance of re-igniting her feelings for him. Yet none the less she sometimes wondered what he was doing, and why he was doing it. And even who he was doing it with.

The fact that she had, as a student, tried to sell a bit of rural and remote Scotland to those who wanted to see it seemed the only qualification she needed to be appointed tourist manager for miles and miles of empty countryside. The salary, whilst not great, was enough for her to rent a tiny cottage within walking distance of the flimsy glass-fronted office where she supervised a single elderly woman during the winter and, in the summer months, a couple of students as well.

It used to be that at the end of each week she would make a few phone calls, look at the number count written down by whoever had been on duty each day in the centre, and fill in a form for onward transmission to her bosses in far-away Inverness, who passed them on – in time – to even-further-away Edinburgh. And in Edinburgh they would be fed into a Scottish Visitor Administration computer in order to confirm what she had known ages ago – that although more and more people were coming, less and less of them were spending time with her and what she offered. Her type of tourism was becoming old-fashioned. So now, was her means of serving it. This year everything was automated. The bell pinged and a little electronic spark shot off to Mumbai, recording one more visitor to the tip of Scotland. A brochure was purchased and another spark briefly illuminated a screen in Singapore or Srinagar. Her phone had ceased to ring, because all calls were rooted to Rajasthan, where people who had never heard of Highland Scotland earnestly advised non-English-speaking visitors on how to find the cathedral in which Madonna was married.

She was more than bright enough to know that soon she would be redundant. Whatever human input was still seen as desirable could be done by phone, or video link, or by a temporary worker from Wroclaw – or even by a cunningly written bit of computer code for, as on-line booking was the flavour of the times, all she now did face-to-face was mollify the bed and breakfast proprietors (inevitably retired from Manchester or Motherwell) who could not or would not adapt and who, like dinosaurs eyeing the darkening ash-filled sky, complained that nothing was being done to help them and their rapidly souring dream of a rural idyll.

"Absolutely," she would nod and promise to pass on the concern, and a computer could easily do that. Though perhaps it would not feel, as she felt, that the best thing they could do would be to write it down and put it in a bottle and throw it into the sea by the little cave below the office, because that would at least mean that if it was found, someone would be interested at least for a moment.

Her depressing thoughts about her future were interrupted by a noise further up the beach. Two kids were playing on a quad bike, driving it along the edge of the water and shrieking as the spray showered over them. They

36

interrupted her thinking and awakened a slight sense, if not of duty, then at least of obligation. She turned back towards the car park, her office and the racks of dusty literature.

As she made her way up from the beach the quad bike roared up behind her. She recognised the two boys, in their late teens, but she was surprised at their choice of music, blaring from the ghetto-blaster tied onto the bike with binder twine. It was the Beatles, the Sergeant Pepper album, a long way in the past even by her standards. And something in it stirred a memory of Donald's little house and a shaft of sunlight on record covers and an unmade bed – and a deep inkling of something else glimpsed or recalled that she couldn't quite place, though it flickered inside her.

But it wasn't about him. It was about the village. Passing the old poet's grave she made the link. When she first came here she had been told a story about John Lennon and the fact that his cousins had lived in the township, or come on holiday there because of their local connections. And so had Lennon.

It was Iain MacMillan who had once mentioned it in the bar, to general merriment and ridicule, but it turned out to be true. The house in question was somewhere over the back from the tourist office, sitting on a hillside above a fence. It had been empty for years, just another croft whose owner earned a living far distant from his roots. When she had enquired about somewhere to stay, she had been told she might be able to buy it, but she had no money and had contented herself with the little rented cottage by the sea in which she now, after two years in residence, jealously guarded her privacy.

The bell on the door pinged as she opened it. Mary looked up from the counter, but didn't bother to put away the woman's magazine she was flicking through.

"Busy " asked Susan.

"What do you think " replied Mary, with a gesture that took in the empty office, the revolving display stands that were standing still as usual, and the slightly dog-eared posters only just adhering to the walls.

Susan lifted the counting book. There was one new entry since last night.

"You've had a customer "

"One man, looking for somewhere to buy as a holiday home. It didn't fit with the call centre referral form, so I took the risk and told him to go and see Iain at the hotel. Apparently he has keys now for that house up the back – it seems that whoever has it doesn't want to come home. Oh, and the keys for your cottage."

Susan knew that her landlady was keen to sell but she resented the thought that there might be any interest in buying. She turned to go back out.

"I'll go and see if he's sending anyone up to me. I'll need to tidy up."

As it turned out she was too late. She was lifting the latch of the gate when a tall, well-groomed man came out of her cottage with Iain MacMillan, the local hotelier, garage owner, entrepreneur and fixer.

"Mr Quigley here is interested in buying, I'm afraid," said Iain as gently as he could. "Wants a holiday house, and prefers this to the one up back."

Susan's heart sank. She had grown fond of the whitewashed walls, of the box-bed alcove (was that why she took it) and even of the smell of damp in the added-on kitchenette.

Quigley had a Glasgow accent, polished by money and success. They were introduced, but he was not a man for pleasantries. He addressed his substantive remarks to Iain.

"I'm very interested. In fact I am going to make an offer today on my way back through Inverness. If it can be arranged I'll want it quickly though, as there is a lot of building work to be done and I would like to get some use of it before the end of the summer." And then, with the lack of sentiment that comes from success in business, he seemed to remember that Susan had a minor role in his plans. He smiled unconvincingly at her and said, "Sorry to ask, but could you be out in a couple of weeks It would help."

Iain, a building contract in mind, had obviously indicated that Susan's tenancy was no problem. The offer would be no problem too, as Susan's landlady was canny enough to take a good offer now, even though the market was rising. Better a bird in the hand. Susan briefly thought of fighting, of shoving past them and barricading the door, but that was not Susan.

"Of course," she said with as much charm as she could muster. "I hope you will be as happy here as I have been."

She did not take the proffered hand, and after a few desultory remarks Mr Quigley got into his Jaguar and gunned the engine as he headed off to finalise the deal. Iain perched on the stone wall and offered his commiserations.

"Don't take it too hard," he suggested. "There are other places you can stay. You can have a room in the hotel until the season starts or you could always look again at the house at the back above the fence. I have a feeling it won't sell unless it is pushed, and yon man doesn't seem to want to push it – in fact I would say he wasn't that keen on shifting it, strangely enough. You could even squat there!"

Susan nodded a vague assent to whatever arrangements might be possible. Iain set off back to the hotel, with a commission no doubt secured on the sale, and the prospect of a few more regular customers in the bar during the summer. Susan took a long look at the view, as if for the last time, then closed the door behind her. It wouldn't take long to pack her things, but the day had certainly taken a turn for the worse.

Perhaps there would be no job at the end of the season, the way things were going. Perhaps it was silly to get upset about having to move on from where she had been happy in her type of isolation. But she did not feel like leaving this place and the people around her.

As a city girl she had wondered if she could take to rural Scottish life in more than summer rations. Yet within weeks she had fallen into the rhythmic pattern, content to get her limited supplies at the local shop, happy to socialise in the bar in the evenings, or call on a growing circle of friends young and old to chat, drink tea and while away the winter hours. Those that were born to it often wanted to leave it. Those who chose it were rarely ready to give it up without a struggle.

But she was also a practical girl – Donald had leant on that side of her nature for long enough. If this house was no longer to be hers, she would need to find something else and the sooner the better. So within the hour she was standing in the other house that Iain had the keys for, looking around and wondering if she could find a way of making it her own.

The house was larger than her cottage. Built perhaps in the 1930s, it was a typical two-down, two-up croft house with a narrow wooden stair and a small old-fashioned toilet and bathroom crammed between the two bedrooms. It was dark downstairs, and there was a smell of disuse, though the place seemed wind- and water-tight. From the back kitchen there was a view of a hillside, rising steeply behind. The front windows looked across to the small village – as usual the end faced the sea and the prevailing winds, and there were no windows in the gable. She was surprised that no one had snatched it up yet, although she knew that Quigley was right, as she was right, to prefer the other one.

She wandered upstairs. The dormer roof was low and, as she carefully picked her way across to the small window in the bedroom on the right-hand side of the stair, she stumbled on a loose floorboard, and dropped the house key. Bending down to retrieve it, she noticed that the paper was peeling from the wall. The naked light bulb (necessary even at this time of day for the sun would rarely warm this dark wee recess) cast a harsh glare, but as she glanced away something under the paper caught her eye. It looked like a drawing and she crouched down to get a better view. She edged the paper up, and then up again, until she could see a few inches of what lay beneath.

There was a drawing. Underneath it were two lines of poetry. She gently pulled the paper up a little more, to reveal more writing. Then she eased the paper off from both sides of the exposed gap, opening up more and more of the plaster wall.

There were more words, another picture and what looked like the edge of a cartoon. She moved a couple of feet further across the room, where there was a seam between two pieces of wallpaper and she gently eased each side from the old paper below. More writing, and some musical notation – or what looked like musical notation.

She stopped and stood up. Thinking about what she had seen, she suddenly recalled that this was the house in which John Lennon used to spend his holidays with his aunt. She had been a Beatles fan when she was young, though the music pre-dated her by a decade or more. She had bought the records, then the CDs. And she had bought the books. Books that had drawings and writing just like this.

She tackled another seam about a foot further on. It was just the same – under the paper were words and pictures in a variety of coloured inks. But perhaps not ink – they seemed more permanent, as if whoever had made the

41

marks had used paint or an indelible marker. Did they have indelible markers in the fifties, she wondered And when was all this done

Two thoughts collided in Susan's brain. The first was that no one presently in the village (as far as she could guess) apart from her, knew about this remarkable wall. The second was that she needed to live here in order to work out what to do about it.

She carefully replaced the paper, trying to hide any sign of what lay beneath it. Getting the paper off at some stage would require extraordinary care and until then she didn't want the chance of anyone else knowing what she had found. She put out the light and came down the dark stairs. She locked the door and took the key back to Iain MacMillan.

He greeted her with a smile.

"Good news. I rang yon man who owns that house. He's still undecided about selling, so he will rent it to you for the summer, as long as you agree to get out within a month if he decides to get rid of it. It will be the same rent as your old one, too."

"I'll take it," said Susan. "And I'll move in tomorrow."

"No point in hanging about. You might as well keep the keys."

It was late afternoon when she got back to the office. The doorbell pinged again. Mary had finished her magazine and was idly staring out the window, with a cup of tea in her hand.

Susan looked at the book. Two more since the morning. She raised her eyebrows.

"Two Dutch cyclists," answered Mary. "On their way to John o'Groats. Seem to have gone a bit off-course, and one of them looked half-dead. I took pity on them and didn't make them fill in the forms."

Susan should have scolded her but she had something more urgent to do. She closed the flimsy door to her office and switched on her computer. An Internet search produced hundreds of Beatles sites, and thousands of references to John Lennon. Several had samples of his drawing and his handwriting. They stared back from the screen at Susan in exact reflection of what she had seen not an hour before on a bedroom wall on the furthermost edge of the world.

She looked at articles on pop music. She looked – because the links were there – at visitor attractions, at the hundreds of fan sites, at visitor numbers, even at Graceland. Mary popped her head in at five o'clock to say that she was away home and was locking the door, but Susan carried on searching and reading and noting down information. She was surprised when the phone rang and Duncan Cameron asked her if she was still coming down to the bar to play in the pool competition, as she had promised, because it was after ten and they were all waiting. And what on earth could she be doing working late – did she have a man in there

She told him she would be with them in ten minutes. She switched off the computer and sat in the dim twilight that seeped into her office. It being early summer in the north of Scotland, the street lights were only just coming on and it would be a while before it was anything like dark. Her mind was in a ferment, an experience that she rather enjoyed as it was so rare these days. She knew that she had discovered something tremendous but also something very fragile and potentially very dangerous. Not just fragile in itself, but fragile because of what it offered or might offer to a fragile community. And dangerous for that reason too. It would – she knew – and could become the hub of a tourist attraction that could transform the place. Money would be no object and anyone who bought the house could sell it on to one of a dozen tourist companies for a small fortune.

Then would come the visitor centre, and the merchandising and the tours, and there would be a need for more hotels and shops and petrol pumps. There might even be drive-through burger bars. Even staying in her present job her prospects would be transformed, and that seemed the most dangerous prospect of all. For although she wanted to be saved for a future in this place, she did not want it at the cost of the place itself.

She got up and went through into the main office. In the dark she could see the sea glinting as it rolled onto the headland half a mile away. She let herself out and re-locked the doors, though there was no real need to do so here. Her footsteps echoed as she walked up the street, and she could here the laughter and noise from the bar as she approached the hotel door.

On the doorstep she turned and looked round. From here you could see the whole stretch of the coast, and the lights of a fishing boat (one of the last) somewhere to the north. The stars were dimly coming into view and the slight cold wind whispered past her ears and on down into the other parts of this wild and lovely landscape. An oystercatcher called somewhere to her left.

Everything needed change to survive. She knew that, even in her romantic heart. But what change The change of tourist buses and motorcycles and screaming children towed about by their bored parents

She knew instantly that she must say nothing, at least for a while. She would explore those amazing walls and discover what was there.

And, she suddenly realised, with a shudder of dislike at her dependency at such a moment, she would write to Donald asking for his help in deciding what to do. Even after all this time.

She opened the bar door and prepared a normal smile. The warmth, the conversation and the smell of whisky intoxicated her before she had moved into the light.

5. HERE THERE AND EVERYWHERE

There are people and places you cannot live with, or without. But we try.

Stop a stranger in any pub in the city, and like as not you will find someone who was born and brought up in a distant village or on an island croft. Offer him his ticket home and he will say that he goes every summer and returns after a fortnight thankful that he now lives somewhere else, no matter how deep his attachment is to his roots.

Your conversation will be interrupted by the band preparing to play, for this is Friday night and entertainment is provided to counterpoint with the noise of opening crisp packets and the chiming of the till. In urban Scotland there will be rock music, or the latest street corner band. But if you go to the far western country, soon everyone will be regretting leaving Tulsa, or longing for Santa Fe, for Country and Western rules in our Highlands and not just the younger ones will be hungrily talking of being elsewhere. They even sing Hank Williams songs on the Faroe Islands (in Faroese, and thank you, Ragnar, for singing them to me in your kitchen), so this is not a peculiarly Scottish illness.

Go further, to the wine bars of Soho, or the working men's clubs (they still exist, though the work is different) of Corby or a petty officers' mess in Portsmouth. Somewhere there will be a Scot who claims to be as patriotic as the next man (which is you). Travel to the Caribbean, or to the Australian outback, or to the high-tech paradise of California, and you get not only Scots, but those who think they are Scots, whose clan is Shufflebottom and whose tartan is the hunting Lewinski, but who still claim to hanker for their granny's and granddad's Heilan home.

But none of them are in Scotland, just as none of our internal exiles are in any place to behold the distant Hebrides. Home is the place they don't go to, and which they never ask to take them in. Home is the root that both nourishes and poisons the far distant flower.

But just as those who come from the far parts of our land gravitate inevitably towards the middle, so some of those in the middle gravitate to the edges. Most – the commuters who need a bit of space and fresh air and somewhere to bring up the children – go only as far as they can travel in an hour or so, in their comfortable cars.

But some go much further, re-making their lives in places very different from what they know. Unlike the migrants to our cities, though, they are never completely part of their new home – or only if their descendants survive a couple of generations of rural isolation.

Insecurity is part of the Scottish condition. We come from somewhere else, and settle where we feel least uncomfortable. We belong to places that we only visit, yet we are visitors in the place where we live.

Two generations ago those who are our ancestors mostly travelled no distance at all, from birth to death. Now we travel all the time and get no satisfaction from it.

And how insecure we are in other ways. We have our own languages, but we aspire to speak someone else's. We are the inheritors of untold riches, but we trade them for a mess of pottage. We have made the world (have we??) but will not take responsibility for our own lives.

No wonder our nation is confused. No wonder our principal sickness is lack of confidence. We never stand anywhere long enough to feel secure about what is under our feet. Or if we do, we never stop thinking that somewhere else is where we might rather be, and might be happier if we were there.

"Ah, don't you see?" wrote the Greek Alexandrian poet. " Just as you've ruined your life in this one spot of ground / you've

47

ruined it over the whole earth." Or to put it another, more prosaic, way: you can't get away from yourself. But we all keep trying.

6. WORKING CLASS HERO

Charlie MacKellar had worked hard to get where he was. And he was damned if anyone was going to upset it all now, no matter who the bastards were.

As befits a hero of Scottish toil he did not make too much of his working-class roots except when it suited him. But when the time was right – depending on the audience or the carefully selected and sympathetic journalist – he would open up his well-thumbed and well-ordered memories to reveal a wartime childhood by the dirty lower Clyde, a post-war brush with the steelworks and trade unionism, and then a miraculous escape by dint of talent and a fair amount of arse-licking that took him into local government, into business (local government opens doors, he always said) and then into the House of Lords.

He had found it easy to make money – far easier than working for it amongst the furnaces and the smoke – and easier still to give a little bit of it away to his party and selected party aspirants. There was more than one Cabinet Minister who was grateful for his help at a sensitive time even if it was not acknowledged in the Register of Members' Interests.

When Blair entered Downing Street there had been talk of a government post, but someone had got in first, someone with a little more polish and a little more protection from the Chancellor. But he was not forgotten. The Scottish Visitors Administration was the plum quango with lots of foreign travel and a product that sold itself. When named as Chairman it seemed only what he was due.

49

But, for the first time in his life, his timing had been awry. No one had told him that Scottish tourism had been run by arseholes for most of the last thirty years, and that the air was about to become thick with the fluttering sound of somewhat deadweight chickens preparing to plummet home.

Then there was the little matter of an oil economy that treated petrol as the cash cow for public spending. It didn't matter much in the leafy shires of merrie olde England but it sure as hell did when you were located several expensive tankfuls from the nearest airport. Which of course meant most of Scotland.

The final straw, though, was the succession of foreign and domestic policy crises that persuaded Americans – the key and virtually only market according to the theorists of the SVA – that visiting Europe was likely to lead to either complete destruction on board the aircraft, immolation on one of the pyres of burning diseased animals when you landed or infection with multiple deadly and extremely unpleasant toxins and viruses which daily swept across all but the sacred soil of home.

To date Charlie's tenure in what was meant to have been the comfortable and well-padded Chairman's seat had been, as he frequently expressed it to his long-suffering wife Betty, a "fucking grade-one nightmare". It was particularly galling that he seemed to be the only one who worried about falling figures, endless complaints from the movers and shakers in the tourist business and very offhand meetings with whatever government minister was responsible that week for what his party in office still had the temerity to call "Scotland's number one export earning industry". His staff (as he liked to call them) just went on spending money, claiming expenses and jetting off on fact-finding trips. Sometimes it seemed as if he hadn't seen any of the people who were meant to report to him for months, and when he asked where they were it was always Ullapool or Acapulco – and usually the latter. The only thing that got through to him was the bills for the computer systems these people kept buying.

To add insult to injury he had originally been appointed for three years, and – despite the difficulties – was just beginning to look forward to the last bit of his tenure, probably another one if he wanted it, and then a dignified retirement, when the Scottish Parliament started to show an interest in what he (or more precisely the SVA) was doing, or not doing. He had himself never been particularly keen on devolution, thinking that his party might be going to a lot of bother and self-sacrifice to buy off the separatists when a bit of firmness and a bit more unionism would have served everyone better. But it had happened even though he voted, in the privacy of the booth, against.

Now it seemed that it was all changing, and not for the better. Questions were being asked and critical statements made, even by those MSPs from his own party who should have known better, or who at least should have known not to bite one of the hands that fed them. It was, he said to Betty, "horribly fucking different from what it was meant to be. Who do the fuckers think they are "

For a start he didn't really know any of the idiots who had taken charge. Donald, naturally, but who the hell was Jack, except someone who kept things in order, or was meant to And as for the rest, well the new ones seemed even more mediocre than he had expected and they talked a lot (and in public) about things that they never did and couldn't do. And the people who were meant to keep them straight, to do their jobs for them as it all used to be done in the town hall, they weren't much good either.

In tourism it seemed particularly bad. Minister succeeded minister but whilst the talk got grander the money got less. Yet even with money it was obvious that

51

they were up a gum tree until the world changed, or someone came up with some idea. At times he remembered that it was his organisation's job to come up with just such an idea, but that was not something that ever featured in the work plans, the strategy documents, the blue sky reports. It was all numbers, projections and penetrations.

Penetrations, my arse, he often thought.

The Parliamentary Committee was like an accident waiting to happen. One Wednesday the Industry and Export Committee announced an enquiry into Tourism Earnings. The next day he was asked to appear, with a date set. Nobody but him seemed to be worried. All his instincts – all the years of them – knew they should have been. Yet, fool that he was, he kept saying to himself: this is a Labour Parliament, a Labour Committee, a Labour Country. They won't let Charlie MacKellar down.

Afterwards – long afterwards – he still couldn't bring himself to remember the full horror of his appearance in the slightly tatty splendour of the Parliament's temporary Committee Room 1 (something had fallen off the walls or the roof of the permanent one – it kept happening).

His office had (spitefully he thought) obtained a video record of the awful event, but he had never watched it. Nor had he read the transcript, or the final report. He had let his officials do that – no doubt on a beach somewhere in the Caribbean. He hoped the shock had made them forget to put on sun block. He hoped they burned like hell.

What he could remember were the faces. It had started blandly enough, with the Chairman suggesting he make a short statement about his organisation and its plans. The statement was in his folder and he had read it before – once at least. It seemed fine, full of platitudes, excuses and the odd bit of optimism. The promise of hard-won jam tomorrow, even if in the smallest possible measures, nearly always worked.

But there was this wee woman, he remembered, who had started the questioning. She seemed better suited for working in a burger bar or something, but she had lifted her head, poked her finger and said, "Whit about Glasgow, and they museums "

Culture and heritage was not Charlie's strong point but he had prepared lines in his folder, and one was about the partnership (good word, buzz word) with local tourist boards, and cities and lots of other places. He read the prepared text as if he wasn't reading it.

Yet it didn't seem to work. Halfway through he thought that something had happened to his powers of speech. Then he felt the hostility. He didn't understand. But they understood. It was – he knew it instinctively – his moment of going off the rails.

The wumman didn't stop. She too seemed to have bits of paper in front of her and although his best brains had marshalled all that he had, it was written in a type of foreign language. Hers wasn't.

She knew about falling figures, she knew about how nobody in the Executive gave a fig, or even a farthing, for the untold riches that sat in cupboards in buildings that had seen better days. She knew that the SVA had refused to help, and instead had "invested" in a new Technology Centre, which was already limping towards closure. She seemed to know about everything, and to positively despise anybody who was in charge, particularly Charlie MacKellar. Somehow she seemed to think it was all his fault.

The Convener moved them on. That was worse. There were questions about regulations, subscriptions and employment. It was as if all the carefully constructed edifice that was the SVA (expense accounts and all – had come up) was being battered by a succession of hammer-headed termites, undermining, crumbling, reducing to dust.

There was one smug bastard who went far too far. He was a Nat of course, and he smiled and cajoled and asked the same question again and again. Charlie would cheerfully have ripped his fucking head off, but even as he fought back he could see that they were against him, and he could feel the sweat on his back, and the eyes of the gallery behind him.

Then it was over. He left, he talked to some smirking journalists, his people fluttered about him and didn't speak in the car on the way back. In time the television and radio wondered (too loudly) about crisis, lack of confidence, need to intervene. The Minister asked to see him, and he wondered (too softly) about crises, lack of confidence, need to intervene. He went through it all in a dwam. It wasn't his fault. Really, it wasn't his fault.

And then the Executive civil servants came. One of those "target monitoring teams" or some such. From the first they were difficult. They kept asking for things he hadn't got, or had never been shown. He glimpsed them in offices as he came and went (earlier and earlier in the mornings now, as if just his presence might make a difference). They seemed to be building a case against him, though he still thought himself guilty of nothing. Yet he was a head, and heads sometimes have to roll.

One day they said they were ready. He was ready too – ready to jack it in and throw himself on the Labour Party's mercy. Yet, miraculously, they presented him not with a nightmare, but with a dream – the dream of an escape. They all wanted an escape, of course, but this one was for him as well as for them.

(For, said Charlie to Betty one night when going to bed, no matter what, I am going to be in the fucking lifeboat. No way I'm swimming with the sharks. Their arses are on the line too. I know it. They can't fool me.)

54

They had noticed, they said (smug bastards that they were) that the SVA and the Executive had a joint interest in the Department of Applied Tourism at the University of Seafield along with a commercial sponsor. They had received notification, they said, that the commercial sponsor was in discussion with "Heather Pure" of Lanarkshire with regard to a take-over. They had considered that this take-over might well be in the interests of Scottish tourism, and had sought and received certain assurances about a desire to invest in the future. Perhaps it would be, shall we say, prudent to explore the options with the university. New ideas might emerge that would make a difference. And they would be seen to be doing something positive. So, might a letter be sent Might a meeting be set up Might it be the right time to explore a future

The Minister, they said, was keen on making progress. (So his arse was on the line too, thought Charlie. Good. Whoever he was.)

Charlie knew an escape route when he saw one. He also knew who ran the so-called University of Seafield. He knew Peter Lochhead (smug bastard). He could be pressured. He could find a way out. (You don't get to run a fucking university unless you're clever, said Charlie.)

The money was what mattered and there was lots in Heather Pure. He might even fancy a wee investment in it, through nominees of course.

Charlie could always feel money, or where it might be. He could feel it flowing round him, to protect and preserve. It felt good. It always did.

No fucking sharks this time. Not yet.

So he wrote the letter. No, of course, his civil servants wrote the letter. He signed the letter. A meeting was arranged. Charlie's padded leather seat was safe, for the time being at least.

7. WATCHING THE WHEELS

What could one possibly say about our once-hoped-for, hard-fought-for, common-cause, Scotland-forward, bright-as-a-button, reconvened-after-300-years, brand-new Scottish Parliament that hasn't been said before? Nothing, save to say it again: how people wanted it (except people like Charlie) and anticipated it, but when they got it, it seemed quickly to be not that much different from what they had before. We might have asked ourselves who else had re-discovered their voice after three centuries of being dumb? Who else has stepped on to the stage of the new millennium after the longest intermission in history? Who else had been the Rip Van Winkle of democracies, the sleeping beauty of international politics? And who else could have done it any better?

But after the party, the hangover. Half of us think that it isn't even worth voting to fill the place. That alone speaks volumes. The others are split between those who want excitement, those who want nothing very much, and those who think that all we have to do is shout loudly enough and a bountiful future will be given to us, free, gratis – great to have all that oil and whisky and everything owned by the people.

Our Parliament does some things well – but those are the things we never hear about. It interrogates the likes of Charlie, and holds him to account. Its members – or those that work and most do – beaver away to get houses for people who don't have them, justice for people who are denied it, a chance at health for those who are neglected. They try to right wrongs, and sometimes they succeed. And if they fail, then those wrongs are usually the ones that cannot be righted, the ones that have been left to moulder for years.

But our Parliament is not the only way for us to move forward. The real main purpose of our Parliament may merely be to stop us moving back – to create the space in which we can get on and learn some other lessons. Lessons of confidence, and self-confidence. Lessons about who we really are, and what we really want.

For a start, we are not unique. All over the world there are people who are half free, and half in chains. The big rule the small, the strong rule the weak, and those that are neither one thing nor the other can either sink or swim. We are not waving, but drowning. Yet we could walk out of the sea. Many do. Others are still trying and could teach us lessons, if we would learn.

The problem, as that famous Pan Am poster once almost said, isn't out there, it's in here. It's with us. Those that we elect have the same problems as we all have – problems of small minds, brave hearts, and the unbearable burden of being expected to be the answer, when no one has even yet had the courage to ask the question. And how can you find your destiny when you cannot find your heart?

8. HELLO GOODBYE

It was not, thought Donald as he surfaced from his hangover, a good idea to have tried to forget with drink. Though at that moment he could not remember what he had been trying to forget.

The instant of remembrance came as he lifted his leg to try and start the blood flowing again, the leg having been underneath the rest of a fully clothed him in a chair in front of a glowing electric fire and a television set that seemed to be showing mid-morning television at the time of daylight when he should have been teaching a tutorial.

As it would have been even more painful to settle back, he moved forward, lurched upright and groaned. The groan was, however, better than being sick which he wanted to do, and not just from the however many pints, the wee whiskies, the curry and something else which was probably cigarettes. He wanted to be sick because he knew it was finished.

His two years of being, not famous or rich but at least comfortable were over. His conversation with the Vice Chancellor (he begin to recall it in gory detail, flashes of horror stuttering into his mind like the work of a demon projectionist) had seen to that. There was no big thing, or no big thing he could find. He didn't (it was a vocation that he just didn't have) find big things.

And yet – he suddenly realised – he was going to have to try, if only to prolong the moment of execution. Now he was thinking with the self-deluding lucidity of those who are still drunk, but no longer enjoying it. He glimpsed a chance which might possibly avert the evil hour. He must be seen to be doing something.

He did something. He was sick.

He was sick again on the way to the university – it wasn't far, but it seemed it, and the seagulls were in a particularly evil mood. He was sick once more in the toilet surrounded by concrete blocks that was meant to be the acme of staff private facilities on his office corridor. And he would have been sick for the fourth time if he hadn't fallen into his seat behind a desk that looked as if it had been attacked by a bomb loaded with paper.

He did nothing. For a long time. His secretary was ill – that was her vocation – and the students that should have seen him had long given up being even mildly concerned when he didn't appear. Slowly he tried to concentrate on what he really should do. He should think for a start, and see if there was anything in his mind that even suggested a big thing.

There wasn't. So he started to think if there was anything anywhere else that might suggest it. His eyes began to wander as opposed to revolving aimlessly. There was a pile of paper in each corner which spilled along the walls and out into the room, joining up in places like a tide, rising imperceptibly day by day. There were books, mostly history. And there was his desk.

And there were the correspondence files, bulging out of a battered filing cabinet.

Those of you who write to a purpose, who e-mail with something to say, who keep it brief and have never owned a green crayon, except in infant school, are the rarities. I love you.

There are millions of individuals out there who write all the time. They fill pages, they scribble round the edges, they photocopy and send reams; they even pay to be published so they can say what they know the world needs to hear from them. They sense helicopters in the night, they see into the truth of microwave towers (which are beaming thoughts to a supine population), they list the genealogy that has made them royalty, and sometimes they invent things which will solve the world's problems.

All they need is the audience to hear. Then it will all be fine.

Donald was the recipient of ideas from those people. Think yourself lucky you aren't. It is always dangerous to have your name in the newspapers, or sometimes even in the telephone directory.

But there is more. For, in addition to the addicted, the obsessive and the perpetual correspondents, there is a special subset of letter writers. They are even more annoying because they know – with unfailing certainty – precisely how to do the job that you have trained for or have been doing for half your life. Moreover, not only do they know how to do it so much better than you, they are also prepared to tell you – selflessly and at length.

Some of them, of course, were bound to know about tourism. Some even may have known about Donald.

Donald lurched towards the stuffed files which contained mail from both these types of letter writer. They had, on occasion, been sieved and stirred, but never fully opened, far less explored. He pushed the rest of the stuff off his desk (his neighbouring academics were used to the noise – in fact they were probably out seeking novelty as was their duty). He tumbled the files out onto the rare empty space. And he began to open the letters and read.

Did it take days or hours Certainly it was not hard to skim the cream from the rest, or would not have been if there had been any cream. What he had to find were items that made even the vaguest sense and which could be written up in a way that, whilst not exactly dishonest, was still far enough from the truth to conceal their craziness.

Even with a hangover he quickly rejected the mirrors in space that would reflect more light on the Highlands, thus prolonging both the tourist and the agricultural season. He trifled but briefly with the equatorial ring canal, the digging of which would solve all the world's problems including unemployment and outbreaks of ebola. He consigned to the ever-growing heap on the floor the three claimants to the Scottish throne, including the man trapped in a woman's body who was temporarily held hostage by the Queen.

Earnest advice on how to avoid the millennial Second Coming (it was too late for that anyway, which was one of the advantages of neglected files – sometimes they solved their own problems) was rejected, as were rants of any description about race, sex or creed. He did not attempt further than page 2 of Brother Bertram's thesis on the evils of teaching parts of the body (though he noted with interest that he was number 1,467 in the list of recipients, of whom number 1 was the President of the United States), and he utterly refused to be drawn into any conspiracy theory, particularly about the way in which television programmes gave clues to unsolved Lanarkshire murders.

This left him a shortlist of seven. He had almost rejected the last one just because it was – it happens – written in something like crayon or too-frequently-licked pencil. But the idea that it contained was just sane enough to make it possible to look at. The other six were more conventional, but still wacky. All of them, however, had the potential to be a lifeline at this moment when something (anything) was needed.

He looked at his watch and was surprised to discover that it was now evening opening time. Never a hair-of-the-dog man, none the less he felt by now like swallowing the complete greyhound, followed by a terrier

61

chaser. He scrumpled the letters into his pocket and sought the bar.

A drink later he read them again.

Number 1 made him queasy. He had never thought that there could be so much to write about shit. Somewhere, however, in deepest rural Lanarkshire there was an embryo museum of human waste, or rather an embryo (that word was getting him queasy again) museum of how human beings had dealt with their most personal waste. Yet this was no mad adventure. There was a proposal, there was an account of artefacts (some surprisingly rare ones, apparently) and there was even a business plan. There were premises, and there was passion. Perhaps it could work. The writer certainly knew his country's history. Even the privy and its role in the murder at Kirk o'Field was in it.

A more rational, or less alcohol-fuddled, man would have stopped there and given up. Heather Pure might just be a name for an air freshener, but the marketing mix of soft drinks, clear water and lavatories was not one that could be made, even in heaven. But Donald was nothing if not irrational, particularly when avoiding the responsibilities of real life was at stake. He marked it down for his first visit.

Trying to be logical about the geography of it all, his second was on the Ayrshire coast. In the empty shell of a highly expensive building (Millennium money, no less) someone was trying to establish the definitive centre for the celebration of Scottish festivals. Beltane, Halloween and the Auld New Year whirled about on the page, along with lots of information on clavies, neeps and fire. It was worth a look.

Number three was further north. It was boats, and ferries, and pier timetables, the stuff of the Clyde-based anorak and obsessive. But it seemed to have already attracted some support – there was even a letter of commendation from an MSP – and the seaside always sold (though not in Seafield, he thought ruefully).

The mountains were next: snow, or rather the lack of it. This was topical and contemporary and the Vice Chancellor would certainly be interested. But the idea seemed so strange and the letter so oddly blunt that Donald had it marked already as an also-ran.

Then to the North-East and the woman who stored ectoplasm. Helen Duncan, eat someone else's gauze out, this was a spiritualist whose time she predicted had come. She communed with the Scottish departed, and they spoke to her in the accents of Dunbar and Henryson. They dictated Burns and Scott. They warned of disasters to come and lamented those that were past. Moreover they left her with bits of themselves. The dead who gave up their dead toe nails. But she was proposing to run a tearoom too, and her writing paper was nice.

The penultimate was the longest shot of all. It was the licked pencil piece of paper, which had a sort of slimy trail on it and which appeared to be torn from an almanac or year book. There was little detail but it seemed to imply that there was a cache of long-lost Beatles songs hidden somewhere far away, and that it could be found and made much of, if sums of money were exchanged. There was no name on it and no location. It gave a phone number and it smelled strongly of (he knew the smell from the Western Isles) sheep.

Donald was nothing if not at times a realist. He would have believed anything if there was a sign, but in the matter of long-lost Beatles songs in the far country there was not a sign to be seen. Even the word "Beatles" was misspelt, by something – he was certain now – that must have been a much-salivated-over pencil. If this was true, then anything was. And he feared that nothing was. So number six would just make weight in the final report, and perhaps be the escape route (the buying of more time) if all the others came to nothing.

The seventh was bound to succeed, though. Admittedly it had a stamp of quality and honesty that was rare (no, unique) on the shortlist. Admittedly also it was not the type of thing that Hi-Fizz was likely to go for. But he wanted to see it, and see it he would. Perhaps something could be done.

Actions speak louder than words. Donald achieved neither that day, but he resolved that the next day he would inform the Vice Chancellor's office that he was off to see the prospects which he had already shortlisted as potential big things. If he could come back with something half-decent then all might be averted. And he might learn more than he had ever thought he would know about shit, ethereal presences and even neeps.

Donald ordered another drink. He drank it. He would have had a third but even he could not take such damage to his constitution. He stumbled home, with the light already going. He pushed his door open and tripped on the step. He cursed and pushed the door mat back with a thump.

Under it went the letter. Susan's letter.

Donald made it to his bed that night. He slept. The next morning he shaved and washed and packed a bag and went searching his country for what he needed to preserve himself, even the bits of himself he no longer liked. He stepped onto the mat, and off it. The letter stayed where it was.

Such is life.

9. ACROSS THE UNIVERSE

No story can be told, not even a true one, without finding coincidences hanging on every tree, or pushed under every doormat. Scientists, who are wrongly thought to be supra-rational beings (they have been known to have messy lives too) know that coincidences happen, because life happens. They call it chaos theory.

It goes something like this. A gentle, soft, so brightly coloured butterfly flutters its wings in the garden of the mperor's palace. There is a susurration in the grass and the breeze blows up into the sky.

Something forms. A molecule is shifted. Microscopic ice covers a microscopic piece of dust that the butterfly's wings have disturbed and which has been carried miles from home. Then it happens again. Tiny movements build into huge processes. vents of no significance (the mperor's concubine disturbs a sheen of dust on a priceless pearl box, an ancient peasant coughs in his dirty threadbare blanket) occur every millisecond. Huge processes go on for aeons. The sky shifts and stirs. Clouds build and move. Somewhere over Africa thunder is heard and an antelope runs from itself. On a sailing ship, far out to sea, a squally shower lifts the canvas and fills a bucket with rain.

In an office with a ceiling fan in the Caribbean, the window is open. A man looks up from his charts and predicts a storm. The beautiful blue rises and falls with long and lazy waves. The sand is disturbed.

A vortex builds where no one is. It is massive and it rises. It hurtles towards the islands and lashes them bare. People hide.

The sale of flashlight bulbs in Florida reaches a ten-year high (and someone makes a hefty profit, but that's capitalism). In moments the roof of every second house reaches another high, but a more costly one. Children are wide-eyed and scared and their parents worry for their lives as well as worrying about the insurance. The more mercenary (there are always those) calculate their profits and losses. Families in cellars clutch each other and expect a grim and noisy death. Stop lights hang from wildly swaying cables. Somewhere nearby a looter in a rain hat plunders the abandoned buildings. Corpses float on inky water.

And then it passes. The sun comes up on mud and trees and a boat sitting outside a department store. In the cold Atlantic a ship sinks, but the day is almost over. And above it all, where the ice molecule has melted, God's anger fades away.

Do not blame the butterfly. It is probably already dead, eaten by a gaudy bird in mid-flight. The mperor perhaps (or his gardeners) should have chosen another location for the bush whose flower the butterfly wanted to suckle. The frost might have taken the flower and removed the temptation from the butterfly. The pearl box could remain unbrushed, and the peasant die silently in his sleep.

In fact the mperor himself might have decided more wisely to spend that day indoors not looking for anything but himself. None of it would have made any difference, or perhaps all the difference in the world.

Where I sit just now the thunder has started. It will rain but not because of our butterfly or the mperor. It will rain because it will rain and then it will be dry again.

Just as we look for significance, we look for coincidences. Indeed coincidences are our significance. Beethoven died in a thunderstorm, as if that great mind, full of noise and wonder, was releasing itself into the atmosphere and returning to it elements of fury. Or did the heavens themselves arrange to welcome him with a thrilling drum roll?

Do not get too gloomy. Acceptance of things is better, in the end, than raging against them. Chasing coincidences is not the same as chasing significance. Significance is found by looking straight and true and not flinching. It is the scent of the rose and roses are no coincidence. They grow because the ground is tilled, the stock straightened, the grafting done, the roots fed and the sharp pruning knife never resisted. They prick us to tell us that they are real and to encourage us to make them better. They are worth the working.

10. WITH A LITTLE HELP FROM MY FRIENDS

Even after she had moved into the house Susan was reluctant to start on the process of revealing all that might be there.

She chose the room with the wallpaper as her bedroom and, as the place was unfurnished, she made a trip to Inverness with a borrowed van that Calum had got hold of, to buy what she needed.

Calum was just one of the boys she drank with, went to dances with, walked over the moors with and generally went about with. There had been one or two romances in her life since Donald, but she had almost shut down that part of herself in the last year, having sex on occasion with tourists who chatted her up late at night and saying goodbye to them the next morning with fewer regrets than they had. One had tried to come back to see her, had written to her, had pledged undying love, and she was hurt for him, but not for herself.

Calum, she knew, would make love with her like a shot but it wasn't worth it. She liked just sitting with him in his car or driving with him in this van to Inverness and having him helplessly worry over whether this bed was better than that bed and if the man in the store thought they were engaged or married.

Getting the furniture was only a day's work (though another notch in her overdraft, which she also tried not to worry about), but another day was spent putting it together, working out the instructions which were always in Swedish and which – to everyone except a clairvoyant – were as vague as hell about the difference between screw B and dowel C.

This lot was particularly hard. A guide in Gaelic with drawings in cuneiform would have been easier to follow, even given her rudimentary command of the language. Flange Z did not appear to be in line with hole X and whilst Calum struggled, Alan attempted to use a hammer to introduce the pair. Mairi then had to use superglue and masking tape to re-attach the bits of misshapen metal whilst the others searched between the floorboards for nut W, a term that then got applied to poor Willie because he spent ten minutes tightening it the wrong way.

Eventually, as it was all being finished, she went to pick some wild flowers, unfolded her clothes, found a length of cloth that would do to drape an old table by the kitchen window, and generally brought the house back to life.

The only thing she was very careful about was the wall in the bedroom. She thought long and hard about how to keep people away from it, and eventually came up with the idea of ensuring that the first thing that was built was a large and rather ugly wardrobe, which was then put right over the small bit of peeling wallpaper that could still be seen. She supervised the operation, grabbing a hand when someone wanted to start pulling the paper off.

"I'll not be here for too long," she said. "No point in making a mess I'll never be able to repair."

The second night they all sat and had tea in the kitchen, mixing wine and chilli. The place felt better, and she lit a fire in the tiny stove, bringing peats up from her old stack. Calum would get the rest in the morning.

Alan was the one who said it.

"We are having a party in a famous place. Famous for here, anyway," he blurted out with that self-satisfied

69

look he always had. (Alan was a friend of Calum's, not hers, she found herself thinking.) "They say one of the Beatles – that Lenin one – stayed here with his auntie once. Do you think he left anything behind "

"I doubt it" said Susan.

"What could he have left " asked Mairi. "Like letters and things and bits of music perhaps " She swung her legs from the new bench seat, knocking Alan briefly on the knees (he liked that). "Let's hunt for them."

Susan stood at the door and calmed them down. She distracted them by carelessly pulling the cloth from the small table, clattering a bottle to the floor. Then it was all tidying and sorting and back to drinking and some conversation about her famous house and what it would mean. Conversation was fine, though she played little part in it. Searching was another matter.

It was the early hours before they left. She waved them away into the gloaming and then, having locked the door, she tiptoed up the stairs and easily pulled the wardrobe back, for she had not yet filled it and her clothes lay about the room on the painted floorboards. She gently lifted the paper, reminding herself of the practical instructions she had found on a house restoring site on the Web. She laid each small piece in a plastic bag and then in a box. And bit by bit a corner of the wall came alive.

It was just as remarkable as she remembered it. More so with a stronger bulb in the light socket. There were bits where the plaster was pockmarked and little dribbles of dust sloughed gently to the floor as they were touched. But most of it was intact, and not made, as she had originally thought, onto a layer of old paper but directly onto the surface of a wall which had been distempered at some stage.

There were lines of poetry, there were drawings – including one of the house she was in – there were snatches of music: there was even what appeared to be a whole song

70

though it went further up the wall than she could reach at the moment.

On first and even second examination it seemed all to have been done about the same time – the colours of the markers (were they markers) had faded a bit but all to about the same degree so that it was not as sharp or bright as it probably had been when first drawn. There were no dates to give any clue and she supposed that it would take a Lennon expert to identify themes or ideas that would place it. There was, she was thankful to see, no reference to Yoko Ono – far too early for that – and only one reference to another Beatle. The word "Beatle" didn't feature either, though there was a drawing of something that looked a bit like one.

She was falling asleep on her feet, so after a couple of hours she picked up the box, almost full now of fragments of paper that might be needed when the restoration started. She carefully swept up the dust and very carefully moved the wardrobe back. She made sure it didn't quite touch the wall, though now she could see that she had disturbed an area that was almost bigger than the wardrobe and taking more off would make what was behind visible at least in part. She would worry about that later, she thought, flopping into bed, putting off the light, and eventually drifting into what was a surprisingly dreamless sleep, though Donald was in there somewhere.

There was no letter from Donald the next morning. Nor the next morning. She didn't want to e-mail him because she knew he never read his e-mails in the university and they wouldn't be secure anyway. Donald didn't have a computer that he used regularly at home – or rather not one that worked in the way that everyone else's worked. His, he believed, hid messages from him and spent the night contentedly munching his work. He did not trust it.

She solved the problem of the wall by pretending to decorate. She borrowed ladders and she hung a big sheet over the whole area. Calum wanted to help her, but she refused (which hurt him) and for a few days she settled into a routine of work, a drink in the pub and then home. She claimed that she felt tired, and people talked about it and worried, but she seemed fine to them. They wondered if she was in love, but they couldn't thing of who it might be. Sometimes one of the women in the village would turn up and drink a cup of tea and go away more worried still, because everything appeared entirely normal.

So whilst elsewhere Donald was tearing his hair out (what little he had left) and looking at shit and unworldly emanations, Susan was uncovering a treasure.

Eventually she could see the whole thing. It was not the full wall, but there were bits on most of it. Some – particularly the bits to the left – looked as if they had been done later, for the writing was slightly different and the subjects were not the same. In total there must have been over fifty individual items, from a quick scrawl to that complete (or almost complete) song. She lay in bed and looked at what was, to all intents and purposes, a cave painting full of significance and meaning but from outwith her experience. If she had not known who it was by, it would be graffiti, though very elegant and thoughtful graffiti. But because it was by him, it was priceless.

The price was the first thing that made her start to plan. She imagined what would happen if the house caught fire and she was the only person in the world who knew about it. That way lay madness. She thought about buying the house but she knew that she could not afford it and if she rushed to purchase it, that itself might arouse suspicion. It would also give Calum and others the thought that she wanted to stay there for ever, and she had never thought, ever, about ever, except during that summer with Donald.

And anyway even if she could raise the money, she didn't want it like this. That would be cheating.

The secret that she had started to burn within her. What had been exciting began to be a burden. Sooner or later she would have to tell someone.

The choices were limited. She had tried Donald and there was no point in trying again (though she wouldn't give up on him, she thought to herself with a start). None of the girls in the office would know what to do, and Calum was a non-starter, as were any of his friends. She knew the only local minister by sight but he was Free Church and had probably never even heard of John Lennon. Anyway she was not a ministery sort of person and he was highly unlikely to be a ministery sort of Beatles fan. She could ring Lucy or Leonie, or any of her friends in London and Edinburgh, but they were not there to see it and, whilst they might believe her, equally they might not. Not her parents. Definitely not her parents.

She had once caught Iain MacMillan looking at her in the bar and she wondered about him. He was about fifty, lean and fit, always working, with a ready laugh. He was rumoured to have affairs but no one would ever confirm to being one of them and it was a small place – somebody had to know. He did not get on with his wife, they said, and she kept herself to herself. In fact Susan had to think if she had ever really spoken to her.

It was obviously going to have to be Iain. He was an entrepreneur, he would want to make money, but he was not insensitive. He was also local and he would understand the dilemma. Most of all she thought that he wouldn't deliberately – or even accidentally – try to stitch her up. He would think, and she needed someone to think.

It was easily arranged, even if the gossips thought that Iain visiting Susan in the twilight of a still evening when the sky was tinged with orange and blue was a little out of the ordinary. She went down and told him she had a problem in the house and needed his help. He said he would send someone up tomorrow. She asked him to come himself that night and he looked at her again.

"OK, lassie. Half an hour."

She was friendly when he came, and he was uncertain. She led the way up the stairs – there was something quite sexy about thinking what he might be thinking and she made a mental note of that. She stood in the centre of the room and pointed at the sheet that was covering the wall.

"My God, that's a mess – what have you been doing " he asked.

"Just look at it," she said, and gently slid the end of the sheet onto the floor.

He looked. And once more. And then to her. And then once more at the wall.

"What is it Vandals What on earth "

"Remember the history of the house. They're by John Lennon. And I am sure – I've checked."

He was a clever man but it took him a minute or two. He sat down on the bed and looked at the wall again.

"My God, they are worth a fortune. This house" (he looked round) "is worth a fortune. You had better buy it, lassie, and now."

It was the right reaction. She kissed him on the forehead and led him down to the kitchen where she poured him a dram and told him the story. He listened but didn't speak. Occasionally he smiled.

Then he told her another story. Of how he had been told years ago that the boy that used to come to the village had become the tousle-haired, famous, infamous, bearded and lying in bed, pictured standing naked, Oko-inspired, inspirational himself and suddenly dead John Lennon. Of how Angus over in the glen had once told someone that

Lennon had left things behind in the house and how they would be worth a king's ransom. How not so long ago someone in the bar had told the story again. And how, when he had rented it to her on behalf of its faraway owner, he had wondered for a minute if it was meant to happen, and if she would find whatever it was that the house still held. Never, of course, thinking that she would.

And he said something else.

"There is no way of keeping this in, lassie. If I don't talk, you will talk. Or you will have a boy back, and he will talk. Someone will find out and then it will all be lost. If you want the house, I will lend you the money. If you don't, I will buy it myself and make sure you have something too. But whatever happens it is all going to change now."

And then he took off his jacket, put it on the back of the chair by the table and stayed because he needed to talk to her. And to himself.

Afterward the gossips could not contain themselves. It was well past dawn before Iain left the house, though he and Susan had merely sat opposite each other and drank whisky and then tea and then whisky. That's not always adultery.

He talked to her of the place and what it meant, he told stories about it and he brought to life people who had lived here before he or his parents were born.

Like all Highlanders he had been away. He had lived in Glasgow, he had made money, he had enjoyed his youth. But the place called to him every day. When the salmon were running he could see them splash on the wall he was painting in a city flat. When he heard the weather forecast he felt the gales of wind crashing in on him and the slates shake. When it snowed he imagined the view from the hill across the village, white and cold and clear.

In the summer he would come home for a fortnight and stay with his mother, and walk on the dunes and drink beer with the boys he had been at school with. In Glasgow he married a girl from the next village but she was different – she wanted away and she did not want back. And when he came back she came with a heavy heart which had led to problems. Now she had driven the hatred back into herself, and out onto him.

"Not that I didn't deserve it, you know. I have been in love a few times, if that is what they call it. And I have never regretted such things."

More than ten years at home and he had done well. He was good at seeing chances. The garage had been what he started with – the hotel was a bonus. Building came naturally and there was a need. Now he employed people and he drove a big car, and he went to the city and stayed in a good hotel. He still liked the city, but he wouldn't want to live there. He wanted to live here and to be part of what he had become even before he was born, because it stretched back who knows how far.

But he was not entirely happy. He had discovered that some years ago, and whilst he was jolly and pleasant and got on with people, and whilst he was admired and respected and even liked – he still felt that there was something missing in his life, something still to do. It had begun to gnaw at him and make him restless. He thought that explained the women.

Was he hiding from the world Of course, a little. But he was also carrying the world onward, shouldering his decaying bit of it because he loved it and it was him.

Yet it was decaying. It was dying, and he with it. His language was hardly spoken at all by the young people and his culture, such as it was, was tired and frozen and unapproachable. In any case, if this place were to stagger on it needed more than that. Maybe some things needed to die, though he did not feel that when he heard songs, or talked

76

to the old people in the bar, or read some of the poets who had distilled the language for his century.

Sometimes he counted the ruined houses as he drove to the nearest town. Then he counted the holiday homes, and the places where old women or old men lived alone. The numbers kept getting bigger and no one seemed to know what to do about it, or even if anything could be done about it.

"Tonight, lassie, you are hearing my life. And you are the only one who has ever really heard it."

Inside him he knew that nothing would change, it would just slowly decay. And yet he still hoped.

Perhaps this was what he had hoped for. This would, undoubtedly, bring people here, and bring money, and although it would not save his race or his tongue or his country it gave this place a new purpose and might give him one too.

Or would it Would this in fact be not the beginning, but the end. He sometimes wondered if he could live without money and if that would make him content. But he knew he wouldn't. So to make more of it might just make him more restless. Even though he needed (he thought) and the whole place needed, the money and excitement and new chances this would bring.

They circled round the problem until, around dawn, he jerked himself fully awake again after a period of long silence, and stood to go. She wanted to kiss him again, but he turned to the door as if he was thinking of other places but here. Then he paused and looked at her.

"This may have to happen. People will know. I will say nothing for a day or two but I will find out the price of the house. Take care of what you have and take care yourself. It will not be our fault if we get this wrong. But a bit of me is very excited indeed, while another bit of me wishes it had never happened!"

He left the door open and she stood by it in the half-, just coming, light, looking down towards the village. He had turned across the track below the fence when he looked back and waved and then he was lost to sight.

It was like saying good night to a lover after the first act of love when you do not know if there will ever be one again. But she grieved for more than him. She grieved for what would happen here and how the narrow lane that led to her cottage would become a car park

She stood by the table, holding her glass. She could not bear to go up just yet and see what had brought them to this.

11. TOMORROW NEVER KNOWS

Think about our history for a moment. Not the who bashed who, who won what, type of history you were taught at school and either loved or hated, but the real history, the history of who we are and how we got here. And where we are going, because history is about the future too.

Ages and ages ago the sea gave us up to the air. The rock came and it broke, and flowed and fractured and it rose up and fell and slowly it became this land. The land became green when it wasn't white and covered in snow and ice and invisible beneath its frozen load.

Ages passed. The sea ran over it and the lochs emerged. Near-naked things scuttled from the undergrowth, startling the scuttling non-human inhabitants who until then had had only mammoths to be afraid of.

The problems started. Our ancestors, those people who seeded you and me (though parts of us came from different places, the process is the same) stood up, walked, grabbed each other by the hair, found out the difference between sex and love, looked at the stars, were afraid of the moon, and gradually got on with the process of living.

They did it here. Against this backdrop. These hills framed them, these rivers ran over their dirty feet, this bog sucked them in and sometimes spat them out. They gathered things on this shore, they took these animals and made them work for them. They shivered in snowfalls, basked in the sunlight. Here.

We are what happened to us when we did not know it. That, and those who were also shaped by it, shaped us. Our parents and their parents, and all the parents before that fought in dark houses and then made up and made us. Our brothers and sisters chided us, and that made us in a different way. Our friends betrayed us, and that made us too. Our streets and our landscapes upbraided us, and that made us. We thought and we learnt, and we were further made – just as you are being made (a little made) now by reading this, whether you like it or not.

We became who we are. And as we belonged to it, it belonged to us. It was not a choice, not a wilful act. It happened because it happened. This is reality and we need to live with reality although few can do it all the time. You cannot be concerned about the people of this poor, wee, frightened little country that think (alas) that they are doing so well, without being concerned also with what gives them breath, that holds them and that made them. It is all around you.

12. A DAY IN THE LIFE

Donald's first problem was transport. A man who cannot fully master his shoelaces will almost certainly have problems with driving. As he had never found it necessary, particularly on a small island – the postbus service was adequate – he simply resolved the issue by never learning to drive.

If you drive it is hard to imagine what it is like not to drive. If you have a car (and you probably do, book-buying demographics being what they are) then the problem of imagination is even worse.

You want to go from Seafield to Dumdoratt in Lanarkshire You drive. Out of Seafield, down towards Edinburgh, across the Central Belt (listening to Radio Scotland on the way in case of problems at the Castlecary Arches), left on the M73, down onto the M74, past Hamilton and onwards. Two and a half hours and it's a dawdle.

But if you don't drive You take a bus to the railway junction (the railways always went where the landlords wanted them to, like the forces of good order which they are). You board the train which is late and crowded and you won't get a seat. You change at Edinburgh. You miss the connection which is meant to be every half an hour, even at this time of day. You wait an hour. You travel to Glasgow in a carriage that smells of stale chips and which is full of psychopathic-looking neds, drunk wee men and women in anoraks with cans of Special Brew. You change stations. The train smells worse and it stops at every hole in the hedge, except there aren't any hedges, only walls. When you get to the douce wee station at Lanark you wait for a bus. It came yesterday. You hail a taxi. You are driven.

Donald's day was spent getting to Dumdorrat, after screwing a few pounds out of the Vice Chancellor's secretary as emergency expenses and cashing the chit in the University Finance Office, where the sniffy girls scented from him the seedy aroma of incipient financial failure.

He arrived in rain, and as he had not phoned ahead (mobile phones were also one of his problems), there was nobody in what looked like a huge old shed that he was assured by a scowling and almost unintelligible local was, indeed, the address of a Mr Merryweather, now retired.

He knew he had come to the right place as he prowled around what he assumed to be the backyard. There was a mountain of porcelain of all shapes and sizes and some – as he looked closely – that seemed of no recognisable shape or size at all. There were funny-looking tubs of ancient vintage, pipes, connectors, bends, what looked like ancient urinals and a gilded box like a sealed Byzantine telephone kiosk sitting on its own in the middle of the debris.

His enquiries were interrupted by a car door slamming and a dog barking. The barking came rapidly towards him until it metamorphosed into a huge black and malevolent dog which tore round the corner of the building at a rate of knots, braked, growled and then began to move forward more slowly. He backed off, looking for something to throw. The telephone kiosk seemed to beckon, so he got behind it and peered out. Standing about ten yards from him was a man whom he presumed was Mr Merryweather and who was holding the dog back by its choke chain, with what appeared to be superhuman effort.

"Yes. What do you want " barked an English accent, which reminded Donald of a non-commissioned officer in a post-war comedy. Estuary English gone military, he thought.

"I am Donald Keays," he said, forgetting that he had only had a letter, not an introduction.

"Keays I don't know a Keays. Are you from them "

That is always the worst question to be asked in such circumstances. The listener knows immediately he is dealing with a madman, impervious to reason, yet he does not know who "them" might be – the Revenue, the council, toilet thieves or even aliens. How can he say he isn't. He might be.

"I am from the University. The University of Seafield, Applied Tourism, You wrote to me."

That was also the wrong answer to give. Mr Merryweather beamed and relaxed in relief that his life's work was not about to be snaffled or impounded. Freed from the restraint that was strangling it, the dog bounded forward and knocked Donald down. With the telephone kiosk. Into the pile of ancient sanitaryware.

Afterwards they sat in the kitchen and Mr Merryweather apologised. The dog wouldn't harm a fly, of course, he was worried about spies, of course, you can't be too careful, of course, here let me see if we can get the mud off that, of course you will stay the night, is that another bit of porcelain , never mind, it will mend, of course, now come on, I have much to show you.

He had. Donald spend that night and then the next morning learning about shit apart from when he was trying to sleep in a dingy barracks, illuminated only by a bare light bulb. Or learning about "waste", as Mr Merryweather called it, "something we all have and we all have to ensure is passed away". In the brief time that Mr Merryweather left him alone, he was given things to read.

Donald had a sneaking admiration for real eccentrics. People of passion excited him, because he avoided most – but not all – of his passions like the plague these days. Mr Merryweather (retired) was a man who remained – despite everything – brimful of enthusiasm, conviction and certainty. His passion had just taken an odd course, perhaps because of late potty training, or an experience deep within him that had happened at the age of five when perched on a "Thunderbox" (1911 vintage, made by Shanks in the last year of their Chichester factory) in his parents' home somewhere on the wider reaches of the Thames.

Donald had never seen so many things piled into loose boxes, crammed into byres or shoehorned into sheds. Here was the outcome of a lifetime of collecting items that no one else wanted and it was vast and impressive and mad. But Mr Merryweather was a man of method. It was catalogued, it was researched, its provenance was known ("almost certainly the water closet used by Garibaldi during that night he spent in Selkirk. An unusual design") and he had grafted on a passion for Scotland which meant that Scotland had become the focus of his ambition to share these matters with the world.

He was also an accountant, a man who once had some money. He had a business plan, he had talked to consultants, he knew that a re-created ride through a Victorian sewer, complete with smells, would be the centrepiece of his visitors' experience. All he needed was approval – that and the cash that he had unwisely spent acquiring but not displaying.

Donald knew from the moment he had walked into the courtyard that this was a fool's errand. He knew it when he was hit by the dog, when he sat in the kitchen, when he tried to sleep in the lumpy bed, when he walked between the piles of things that sprouted everywhere. But he didn't say it. He took his leave around lunchtime, assuring Mr Merryweather that serious consideration was now being given by the luminaries of the University of Seafield of the ways in which they could – in partnership – bring his ideas to reality. He accepted a lift back to the station, and he waved cheerily from the carriage window as the train began to move.

Then he put the letter in the back of his bag and tried to forget about it. Six to go. And all, he feared, pointless.

The journey to the West Coast was shorter, or would have been if trains went directly there. But the days of Muirkirk station, of halts at Tillietudlem and Braidwood and even Glenbuck, of the lines that were full of wagons in the night, carting the horticultural produce north and south, east and west, so that it could be sold in the morning in London and Belfast, or the coal so that it could be burnt in Birmingham or Bristol for the greater good of industry, if not lungs, were long over. The viaducts were dismantled or fallen, the tracks ripped up and built upon. So it was back to Glasgow, and then down to the coast, through one of Paisley's many stations (though none for the airport, it being an illogical sort of country).

When he thought of Ayrshire (which he hardly ever did) he thought of industry and grime, a bit like a larger Lanarkshire. But then when he went there (which he did even more rarely) he was always surprised by the wide open fields, the long views and the rolling countryside, which put him in mind of Ireland. And of course there were the douce wee towns by the seaside: arthritic Ayr, prim Prestwick and tight-lipped Troon. It was to one of these that he was bound, where public money had erected a fine new edifice to show off Scotland's electronic past, present and future and which now was closed, as public money had not been forthcoming to actually make it work, and private money knew a drain on the wallet when it saw one.

He almost missed the station, lulled by the motion of the train into a reverie in which he was not traipsing the countryside fighting for his future, but instead back on the island, sitting by a burn with the sun in his face and the day stretching long behind him. It was the clash of brakes and the lurch of the carriage that woke him, just in time to clamber out and to wander down the hill towards the town.

"The E-Centre", as it had been known, stood out on a promontory, beyond the harbour. The signs still pointed to it, but when he got there the car park, carefully laid out in coloured brick, had weeds growing through the cracks, and the stretch of glass doors at the front were firmly locked. He wandered around the back until he found a fire door flapping open, and having knocked and then shouted, he tentatively made his way into darkness.

That was a mistake. After a corridor that was illuminated only by the light coming from the swinging door, he turned a corner and stumbled into blackness. He waited a second to let his eyes adjust and then discerned, across what seemed a huge expanse, a light which he thought must be in a balcony office, given its height. He started to move towards it, feeling his way gingerly, conscious of some movement to his right, as if of a large thing swaying gently in a breeze.

He had made about what he thought was half the distance when his foot snagged on a rope or cord or cable. He pulled free, but immediately there was an enormous bang, followed by a flash of light in which he saw (with complete disbelief) a huge figure of Santa Claus falling towards him. He instinctively put up his arms to defend himself, but was overwhelmed and forced to the ground under what seemed to be a massive sheet of some sort of plastic. As he fell, bright lights seemed to come on all around him and when he touched the ground, it gave way in puffs of white – something that seemed to be polystyrene.

(Two falls in two days, thought Donald as he went down, and all in the course of my work. I wonder if I could claim for industrial injury !)

He must have lain winded for a minute or more, beginning to think about what might be broken, when he became conscious of the sound of running footsteps, shouts of "Oh, ma God" and then a scrabbling which pulled the plastic tight over his head, and then pulled it further so that it yanked him over on his side. When it was eventually lifted off he found himself looking up into the face of a huge bearded man and a much smaller woman.

"Are you all right, son " asked the woman, while the man cleared the plastic to one side, muttering "Could he no look where he was goin Now I'm going to have to reload this lot, and it's no as if we have money to burn." She pulled him up, and proceeded to dust him down, all the while asking if he was OK, if he was hurt, if he needed to sit down, if he would like a "wee glass of something or a cup o' hot tea" to steady his nerves.

He looked around and was both mesmerised and horrified. The plastic Santa (now in a heap beside the wall) seemed to have been tethered amongst the most vulgar set of blow-up Christmas decorations he had ever seen: huge reindeer, massive snowmen, hideous malformed elves, many Santas (in various acts of getting into chimneys, climbing out of windows or just grinning) and even a baby or two. They were surrounded by huge assortments of Christmas lights of every kind – flashing, waving in syncopation, blinking, or just shining. Scattered amongst it all were small artificial Christmas trees and fake snow, into which he had fallen and in which he had been lying.

"It's our Winter Wonderland," spat the man. "Our protest against the very un-Scottish celebration of Christmas. You tripped over one of they big air guns you can use to shoot at it, and then ye fell towards the display. I had nae idea I had left it loaded."

Donald had no idea what to say. But the woman had turned him towards the office, and was part shoving, part leading him towards "a nice wee cup o' tea, and a chat, cos you'll be Mr Keays, here about the grant, I suppose". Donald would have wondered about her ability to see into his secrets, had she not been gathering up his papers which must have burst from his briefcase when he fell.

They made their way towards the window on the balcony, though Donald was so stunned by the other things he was now seeing that he deliberately took his time. Beyond the Winter Wonderland was a field of pumpkins and what looked like a mortar set up in order to fire at them. Next to that reeked the largest and foulest smelling pile of turnips he had ever seen, and a workbench on which attempts had been made to turn a tiny part of the turnip mountain into lanterns. The next exhibit was a bonfire, surrounded by what looked like whisky or fish barrels ("The Clavie," said the man proudly when he saw Donald staring at it). Further on still there was a full-sized wicker man and to its left a herd of plastic cows and what looked like an artificial sheep fank.

By the time Donald was seated in the office, that "wee cup o' tea" in his hand, the man was in full flow. "You've certainly taken your time, Mr Keays, to reply to our letter but I am glad that you have at last shown an interest in what we are tryin' to do. I could have telt them, if they had wanted to ken, that there was naethin' at aa in showin' people aa they electric thin's. Bound to fail. But our idea willna' fail. We are goin' to tell the truth aboot Scotland today, and mak' people realise that their ain traditions are the thin's they need to look oot for, no circuit boards and the like."

"Aye, Jim, you're right," said the woman. She said it often from then on, but not much else.

Jim, it turned out, had worked abroad for years. He had pined for Burns Night, St Andrew's Day, black bun and the het pint and every celebration of Scottishness that he could remember or find out about. Yet when he finally returned to his native heath, he was horrified.

"See that first Christmas I wis waitin' for New Year, for Hogmanay, for real Scottish celebration, for first footin' and handsellin', but a' I could see was tinsel and lichts and big blow-up, fat Santas. It fair made my blood boil. And then on Burns nicht, I had to walk for miles to find any event at a', and that turned oot to be a Tory Burns supper wi' a wee Englishman tryin' to read 'Holy Willie's Prayer'."

So, Donald gathered, it had gone on until the final nadir: Halloween. "No' a turnip to be foon, but huge piles of they pumpkins and kids wi' pumpkins made into lanterns. I'm no' having this, I thocht, and then the idea cam' to me – like a flash, I tell you."

Jim and his wife (for that was the wee wumman) had set about looking for a place to teach the Scots about their own traditions. But not just teach them – to make their "blood boil" and to find ways of getting their own back on what Jim called, using clear quotation marks, "cultural imperialism".

So master classes were to be held in haggis boiling, or tumshie bashing. Visitors would be able to shoot the floating Santas and decimate the pumpkins into pulp. Bonfires celebrating Beltane would be lit, and ones toasting Guy Fawkes would be ridiculed. The Clavie, the Biggar Bonfire, the Stonehaven Fire Balls would be lauded, Up-Helly-Aa would be proclaimed, and Common Ridings would be imitated. But woe betide the visitor who observed the wrong bank holiday or who reminisced fondly about Maypoles.

Donald could see a few flaws in the project, but he was not about to discuss them with Jim, whose eyes were afire with nationalistic passion and who had started to show some flecks of foam on his lips, as his story unfolded. It would be neither helpful nor safe to point out that "Heather Pure" was not going to consider for a moment a tourist attraction that would alienate half its visitors and enervate the rest in not only the wrong direction, but the violently wrong one.

When the diatribe faltered, the woman spoke up. Donald opted for the shorter of the guided tours he was offered, pleading a further meeting and much business still to be got through. He took the badly typed and badly reproduced draft publicity material and he thanked Jim and his wife for their kindness in showing him their "fascinating" idea. He brushed aside any question of being hurt or offended by his unconventional arrival and then he walked (as quickly as was decently possible) back through the town and up the hill to the railway station where he asked for a ticket for the first train to anywhere. Fortunately it was going in the right direction, which was back to Paisley.

The train journey gave Donald enough time both to crumple up the woman's letter and to fret again about his journey. Two down, four and a half to go. Perhaps it was his bad luck, but two more obviously unsuitable projects, run by highly motivated lunatics, it was harder to imagine. Would the rest be the same If so, unemployment loomed ever larger, but even that was a less frightening prospect than the Vice Chancellor's anger and scorn.

He looked at his watch. It was already mid-afternoon – too late to visit the next putative big thing. An evening in Glasgow might be the answer, with a drink or two to start it off. The Vice Chancellor's expenses should surely run to that.

13. BABY YOU'RE A RICH MAN

Hiram Heidelberg is the President, C O and sole beneficiary of Hi-Fizz, soft drinks maker to the stars. Hi-Fizz was originally called Heidelberg's Tonic Wine Company, that Heidelberg being Hiram's long-deceased great-grandfather who had the idea of adding sugar, caramel and herbs to fizzy water, just like his own granny had done to make a drink for the children in faraway Berlin. Old Heidelberg, however, believed, or wanted others to believe, that consuming it might be good for you.

To that extent there is no great difference between Hiram's great-grandfather, Hiram himself, and the likes of Jim and Mr Merryweather. They are all high-minded, driven in pursuit of their aims, and out to succeed. The only point of departure is that Hiram's great-grandfather succeeded, and Hiram goes on doing so. Consequently they are rich, whilst Jim and Mr Merryweather remain poor and are getting poorer. Hiram and his great-grandfather sell something that people know they want; Jim and Mr Merryweather try and sell something that people know they don't want.

What is it like to devote one's life – every waking minute, every dreaming second – to an obsession that appears to be without flaw save for one particular: that of persuading another human soul that it is practical, wise and worthy of support.

Hiram in fact is not quite as creative, nor quite as driven as Jim – Jim aims for his dream, Hiram just aims to go on making money, so it may also be that Hiram is not quite as happy as Jim, if happiness is to do with a total absorption in one's tasks.

Yet as year succeeds year it is, of course, Hiram who is more content (for contentment is not the same as happiness). Hiram does not need to prove his ideas work – money tells him that they do, no matter how destructive they are to our teeth and to our well-being. Jim has no proof, indeed much that proves the opposite – but he will not give up. So he will spend his years to the grave trying to make his idea work, or bemoaning (wandering the little town, down at heel, with a minuscule pension) the fact that the world was not ready for what he had to offer. In fact in time he will probably come to believe that it conspired against him and his ideas.

It could be that someone could make Jim's idea work: could attract money, could enthuse the media, could sit through interminable meetings and could, in the end, open the doors of the e-centre to the world. It might even succeed, at least for a while. But Jim is not that person.

How much depends on talent and how much depends on how you dress, and how you speak and who you know? How much is mere luck, and finding the right person to talk to before one talks to the wrong people? How much is written in the stars, or predicted by the spey-wife looking at the child in the crib?

If we knew that, we would know when to bother and when not to bother, when to speak and when to keep quiet. And some of us would stop doing things altogether, stop taking chances and stop running risks. If we did that, banks would go out of business, remarkable things would stop happening, and we would live swamped by the slow tides of dull conformity. And that would never suit us.

So, licking his wounds, Jim will carry on. Hiram, counting his money, will do the same. And if this venture fails for Hiram (as I think it will, even without Donald) then there will be others. And if this venture fails for Jim and Mr Merryweather (which I think it has, even without Donald), then no doubt there will be more Jims and more Mr Merryweathers. No shortage of them, in fact.

14. TICKET TO RIDE

An evening of drink and conversation at the expense of the University of Seafield was always in Donald's opinion worth having as long as he did not have to have it in Seafield itself. Glasgow held enough old friends and enough serious pubs for him to enjoy himself, though in more moderation than usual, for he was slightly weighed down by Mr Merryweather and by Jim, and by the growing realisation that the "next big thing" was as yet nowhere to be found.

His journey today needed some planning. It was easy enough to make his way to his first appointment, but once he had visited the putative "Museum of the Ferry Man" he had to make his way back to where he started and then north. Looking at the map and then the timetables, it seemed that the only way to do it was to take a train to Perth, and then a bus out into the mountains.

He put himself in the mood for a journey with a fry-up in the station cafeteria, for Glasgow still boasted one of these, although it was now a pub as well. He was not averse to the odd cardboard-tasting, fast-food, on-the-go meal, but a real Scottish breakfast when it could be had at someone else's expense was always enjoyable. Then he bought his ticket and settled down to watch the city pass away, to be replaced by the sweep of the flat Clyde mudbanks, which soon were washed over by the widening firth itself.

He had worked out that if he alighted at Wemyss Bay he could just catch the ten o'clock ferry to the pier at Rothesay, from where it would be a short walk to meet Mr

MacKenzie, author of a dozen books on the timetables and vessels of the Clyde, who had now started to collect the things of which he had previously only written.

Wemyss Bay station was a delight: a glass-roofed Victorian structure which let in light but seemed to be larger than the space it enclosed. But when he walked down the long corridor marked "To the Ferry" he emerged onto a pier at which there was not a boat in sight. He searched in vain for a board with a timetable and eventually found a small office with a glass enquiry window. It was firmly shut so he rapped on it, but there was no response.

He rapped again and then knocked on the door next to it. A few minutes passed and then the door opened to reveal a tousled young man in a pullover that bore the ferry company's logo.

"I thought there was a ten o'clock ferry," said Donald.

"No," said the man.

"But the timetable said there was."

"Only on Thursdays every second week in the winter, November, December and January excepted, and then every third week during the Fair," said the man as if the information was known to all but imbeciles. He then made to shut the door.

"When is the next one " asked Donald.

"Eleven o'clock, but it's cancelled: excessive high water. Twelve o'clock might go if the crew are back from break on time. Otherwise it will be two."

The man then closed the door firmly and Donald heard a key turn in the lock.

He was just about to knock on the door again when he heard his name called and turned to see a small man in a raincoat come up the pier. Behind him there was a small steam dinghy, swaying on a rope which had obviously just been tied to a stanchion, and none too firmly at that.

"Dr Keays I'm Alex MacKenzie and I thought I would come and get you as the ferry is a bit unreliable these days: they are trying to prove a point before it all goes out to tender."

Donald wondered if the point they were trying to prove was that nothing was needed so much as a good shake-up of the entire service, but before he had time to say anything Mr MacKenzie was hustling him down the pier and virtually propelling him into the dinghy, whose single funnel was belching alarming amounts of black smoke.

He had taken the precaution of ringing Mr MacKenzie, not least because his last unannounced arrival had been so nearly life-threatening. But he had not expected that this would mean having to cross the Clyde in what appeared to be a bathtub fitted with a boiler.

It took a moment or two to settle in the boat. It rocked, thought Donald, rather close to the water and it wheezed and chuffed as Mr MacKenzie encouraged the engine. Eventually, with a clash of metal, the gears engaged and there was a strange sound from where the propeller was. They started to move, quicker and quicker, away from the pier.

"1923, built at Skelmorlie and as snug as the day she was delivered," said Mr MacKenzie, as if reading his thoughts about the boat, though somewhat more positively than he was thinking them. "Double clinker hull, and Ormorod self-effacing triple-stroke meths-fired boiler. Superb – and rare! In fact there are only three others like it in the world: one in Argentina, one in New Zealand and one on a wee loch in Uzbekistan, fitted with a Kalashnikov for added protection, just here under the cross-spar. Look, I'll show you the photographs."

With that, Mr MacKenzie let go of the tiller and delved into a cloth-wrapped pouch at his feet. The dinghy proceeded to veer wildly off towards the Argyll shore, but

Mr MacKenzie did not look concerned, and continued to rummage, eventually producing a sheaf of faded black-and-white contact prints which he shoved towards Donald, while grabbing the tiller again before the boat turned back the way it had come.

The boat made steady progress. In fact they seemed to be going at one hell of a lick, thought Donald, a lick which was making the water splash very wetly over all of him. Donald glanced damply at the grainy photographs but as he tried to concentrate on them he became aware of a mass of dark cloud that seemed to be moving rather quickly towards them. Within a few minutes drops of rain were falling, followed by lumps and then huge waves of the stuff, sweeping over the two of them and falling into the boat in a manner that suggested that it would not be difficult, nor would it take long, to fill the entire space.

"A wee shower," yelled Mr MacKenzie. "It was forecast, but it will pass." Donald tried to shove the photographs back in the pouch but as he could not reach far enough to do so, he then tried to put them beneath his increasingly sodden jacket. As he did so the wind whipped them from his hand, and blew them into the water. Mr MacKenzie made a dive to grab them, and the boat swung violently sideways, one side dipping into the water.

What happened next seemed to happen in slow motion. Mr MacKenzie tried to right himself and the boat but over-compensated. He fell backwards as the boat rocked the other way, dipping again, but this time not coming back up. More water poured into the dinghy, which, as the rain was still hammering down, was already awash at its lowest level – a level that corresponded to something hot and vital in the boiler. There was a hissing sound, followed by a spluttering sound. The engine faltered and stopped. The water gushed in faster.

"We need to make for the shore," shouted Mr MacKenzie, falling back onto the bench by the tiller, and yanking it so that the boat shot round and headed, with one side still shipping water, straight at the lighthouse on Toward Point. However, it was obvious that they were not going to make it before the boat filled up completely. There were a few seconds of false hope as the land approached, then the boat wallowed a bit, lurched to its side, and water suddenly surged over everything.

The next thing Donald knew was an arm grabbing his leg and pulling. He realised he was scraping along some rocks and the contact between his hand and something very sharp sent a jabbing pain up his neck and into his eyes which he had instinctively closed. Opening them, he saw, amidst the spray and the sharpness of the salt, Mr MacKenzie pulling him the last few inches onto a sandy spit that jutted out from the edge of some fields.

He choked and spluttered and tried to stand, falling back more than once until he could walk up the beach. Mr MacKenzie had staggered up before him and was sitting on a grassy hummock, looking out to a sky and sea untroubled now by cloud and rain. Of the 1923 Skelmorlie steam dinghy there was not a sign.

It appeared to Donald that three visits and three disasters, which variously involved savage dogs, airguns and now shipwreck, was taking things a bit far, especially for a minor academic. But Mr MacKenzie seemed unfazed by his ordeal, and quite unconcerned about Donald, who was dripping wet and from whose hand blood was trickling down on to the pebbles.

"A pity," said Mr MacKenzie. "Aye, a definite pity. She was the last one."

"I thought you said there were three more," said Donald.

"No, I mean she was my last boat. I had five, but they all seem to have come to grief. The *Uranus* sank at her moorings last winter: the drain cock was left open – a total write-off. The *Lucky* went down when I was trying to get sponsorship for the round-Bute race: I should have remembered the rocks by Rhubodoch, but I was bit distracted at the time. The old yawl from the Uist ferry days, well, it just fell to pieces, and I set fire to the *Unquenchable* – an accident, mind, though I have never been that good with a blowtorch. And now the dinghy. A pity, right enough."

Shaking, soaking and frozen as he was, Donald was quick to realise the significance of what he was being told. "So, you have no boats for the Museum of a Ferry Man, then "

"Not one, I'm afraid. I've still got some old timetables, mind, and a few photographs, but boats – no. Not now. And no insurance. And therefore no museum."

Three down, two and a half to go, said Donald to himself after he had managed to hitch a lift to Dunoon, squelching his way in and out of a bemused head teacher's car. He found a waiting room to at least start to dry himself, begged a ride on a ferry that was going to Gourock (it being neither high water nor the crew's week off), hitched again to Wemyss Bay to pick up the bag he had fortunately deposited in the left-luggage office, changed in a smelly toilet on the train to Glasgow, and then set off again almost immediately for Perth, and from there to Glen Loggierait, once Scotland's premier ski resort. However, by the time Donald got there it was dark – both in the theatrical sense and in the physical one. The bus from Perth had wound its way up through the rising countryside in what was a classic "gloaming" until night fell. When it reached its destination Donald alighted outside a hotel built from pine logs, which at least had one light showing dimly through the front doors.

Although mostly dried out, Donald still smelt strongly enough of the sea for the receptionist lounging at the desk to look up before he quite got to her. There was no trouble in getting a room but more effort was required to persuade the hotel to feed him, he being the only guest.

After he had eaten, he rang the number on the ski centre letter and it was answered by a gruff German-accented voice. However, the conversation soon softened the tone and Herr Voigts would be pleased to see Dr Keays, and indeed would come down to the hotel in half an hour and explain to him what it was he wanted to do and why it was worthy of support.

Donald went and sat in the bar, where a fire had been lit for the benefit of the staff, who – even with the addition of the local drinkers – outnumbered the clientele by about three to one. When once those staff would have been Australian or American students who were travelling and working where they could, now everyone spoke with an East European accent. Given the gloomily austere ambience of the place, Donald had a slight feeling of being an extra in *The Third Man*.

The hotel had certainly seen better days. An approximation of what an Alpine lodge would look like to someone who had only read about them in the "Heidi" books but who was, however, inordinately fond of all the worst features of Scottish hotel design (sticky carpets, toilets too far from anywhere, featureless corridors, kitchens whose old smells seeped into everywhere else, bad sporting prints), its furnishings were sagging and threadbare, and its stocks being run down. All the bar attracted were whatever locals existed within a twenty-mile radius and that was not many. Tonight, as every night, a few of them were sitting morosely on stools at the bar.

Herr Voigts, when he arrived, could not have been mistaken for one of them. Though not wearing lederhosen (at least not outwardly), he clearly had them close to his skin at most times. Tall, blond and healthy, he was fired with enthusiasm.

"The snow is gone," he said gnomically once they were seated away from the bar. "A day here, a few days there, but not in the amount we need. No one will come here to ski except for a couple of hours on a Saturday twice a year when there is the weather. We need to change ourselves and make something that people will want to travel to see."

So far Donald thought he was talking to the sanest person he had yet met on his trip. It made a change, he thought, to be sitting comfortably listening to ideas as opposed to being savaged, shot at or soaked.

"What we need is opera. Opera and ballet," said Herr Voigts.

Donald choked on his beer. "Opera and ballet "

"Opera and ballet – and snow!" added Herr Voigts.

The idea was breathtakingly simple. Herr Voigts intended to turn the ski centre into an auditorium – outdoor and indoor. The ski lifts would be re-routed to provide extra seating, high enough to give a good view of the proceedings. Snow machines would be used to generate the real stuff for the outdoor amphitheatre, and indoors there would be the use of artificial snow (a load of which, Donald thought, could be got from Jim at the e-centre).

Then the companies would be invited. Not just Scottish Opera and Scottish Ballet, but Opera North, Covent Garden, Sadler's Wells, the Bolshoi, the Met, and many others. International seasons would be held, and works would be adapted for performance on snow, or written specially for it. "Your James MacMillan – he seems like an imaginative composer. He could write *The Snow Maiden* or something. And there are others – why we Germans have many composers who would jump at the chance. Your

100

writers too would be keen to come on board; I know that Irvine Welsh could easily make *Trainspotting* into an opera on ice, and snow is often mentioned by your bard, Robert Burns."

Herr Voigts was in full flow now. It was very logical: it solved two Scottish problems in one. It gave the national opera and ballet companies something to do rather than simply run up deficits, it was different, and it might attract audiences outwith the cities. Most of all it brought a purpose back to Glen Loggierait: it would become the Bayreuth of the North.

Donald asked if he had floated the idea with anyone else. Of course, replied Herr Voigts. The Arts Council was keen and indeed had already given him a research grant. He was establishing an art gallery too, and might well in time add on a writer's residence and a sculpture park. The ski centre at Glen Loggierait would become an international beacon of creativity: all it needed was more money and that was where Dr Keays could be most helpful.

Donald asked about projections, numbers, catchment areas, and to every question Herr Voigts had an answer. It was thought through, planned, on the move – everything except possible. This Arts Council grant – how much was it for

"A thousand pounds," said Herr Voigts. "I hired a singer and she sang in the snow. We videoed it. The Arts Council say it is great. But they say there is no more money this year. And perhaps next."

Donald knew enough of funding agencies to get the message. A thousand pounds to go away and make no more of a fuss. To try something once to say it had been tried. It was the usual trick, but sometimes it didn't work. It just stoked the fire and built the desire.

And the local council "Obstructive. They are little men, with no vision. They say the roads won't hold the

101

traffic. And they say that I need a different type of licence. But if they obstruct me more, I will just put everything outside on the hill – the whole thing and we will sing and dance there."

Scottish Opera "Small-minded. They say that they cannot perform in the cold. I tell them that they will soon have to, if they carry on losing money. But I have given them a way forward. In time they will take it."

Donald kept asking questions and the answers became testy. After the first thousand pounds there had been no more from anyone. No one had accepted the invitation. No one was buying or biting. And he was sure that Hi-Fizz would not either. Sponsoring the latest black female singer was one thing: sponsoring Herr Voigts and his very white opera was quite another.

Herr Voigts's project was the worst type of project to be faced with, thought Donald. It was not mad, though it was different. Worse ideas had got oodles of money and flopped after a bit. But to invest in it, to sponsor it, to nurture it was the way of madness because there was something just not right – in fact preposterous despite its logic.

Herr Voigts knew what Donald was thinking. "So you are not keen " he eventually asked. And Donald, tired after two days of being assailed, talked at and almost drowned, was honest for once. "It's not that I'm not keen – I like both snow and opera. But my search for something to sponsor makes me sure that this is not it. And there is nothing I can do about that."

So Herr Voigts finished his drink, bade Donald a sad farewell, and went off back to an empty mountain and the prospect of less and less snow and less and less money until it all went bust, and he found a snowier mountain to serve. And Donald, with the taste of too much human hope and human failure in his mouth (not to say the taste of seaweed) and a sinking feeling for once not about himself but about all those people who wanted things that they could not have and would not achieve, went gratefully to a bed which turned out to be as cold as the rest of this windy, though snowless, place in the hills.

Four down, two and a half to go and Mrs (sorry, Madame) McLintock was no sure-fire bet.

The next day was a respite, thank God. The old problems of travelling re-asserted themselves. Glen Loggierait to Meikle Seggart Bus (or hitch) to Perth – two hours though you could do it in one in your own car. Two-hour wait on the platform. Train to Aberdeen (man vomiting from carriage window, toilet blocked, no water on board, twenty minutes spent sitting outside Montrose). Two-hour wait at Aberdeen. Train to Huntly, wait for taxi, no taxis come. Eventually check in at hotel, have a few drinks, have a few more drinks, spend night, remember to ring Madame McLintock – but next morning so that he is not disturbed by her turning up in the hotel bar. Have even more drinks in hotel bar. Fancy waitress. Go to bed alone.

Mrs (sorry, Madame) McLintock lived in one of those remote parts of Aberdeenshire that are only really suitable for people who work in the oil industry, commute in four-wheel-drives and can afford any number of rural cottages knocked together.

Madame McLintock was in and keen to see him. She didn't drive – she probably teleported by the power of mind – but a taxi was found and (Donald learning quickly) was told to return in three hours' time, to take him straight to Aberdeen.

As the taxi turned off the main road and into the drive of an expensive and nicely restored small house, the taxi driver turned to him and said, "You know her "

"No, but I've had a letter from her."

"Hope you don't mind me saying so, friendly warning like, but she's as daft as a fucking brush."

The taxi sped off down the gravel, spraying stones into the shrubbery, and within seconds the front door opened and an elegant, slightly distracted woman offered her hand.

"Madame McLintock, Professor Keays. It is an honour to meet you. I have sensed your presence for some time."

This, thought Donald, was not possible as he had only just arrived – a fact that was borne out by the gradually settling pebbles behind him. But he forbore from saying so.

He walked – though Madame seemed to glide – into a house which was as different from its outside as the consoles of the Tardis were from the blue lamp on top. It was a spiritualist's cave, hung with drapes and ornaments, with dark recesses and scary-looking things in glass jars on stands. And that was only the hall.

The lounge was set out for some sort of communication with the spirits. There was a large table covered in something very fringed and very full of tassels. It was surrounded on all sides by settees as if protected by covered wagons against attack. In the middle there was a crystal ball.

This time it did not take Donald a day to extricate himself. Indeed when the taxi arrived he was waiting for it, hunched by a hedge at the end of the road. Madame McLintock had wished to let him hear the Scottish poets speaking through her. She had conducted him on a tour of her museum, laid out in a converted shed, and full of obviously fake, constructed from gauze, fingers and thumbs. One might have been a penis, but he did not ask.

She showed him spirit writing that had told her to seek a place of towers by the sea, where she would be helped to demonstrate the truth of the other world. She had

104

seen a picture of Seafield and known it was where she must call. She slightly resented the fact that it had taken a year and a half for the call to be returned, but her guide had urged her never to waver.

Donald's assurances about consideration, meetings, time to work through proposals, longlists and shortlists had sounded (even to him) insubstantial. She had looked at him with large eyes and told him that those who had gone before were watching out for him. It sounded like a threat.

He sat relieved but increasingly miserable in the back of the taxi. It was a different driver, who said nothing and the journey was over in 40 minutes, although for the same number of pounds, which made Donald think about the Vice Chancellor again and his scrutiny of expenses. He asked the taxi driver to make the receipt out for 50, split the difference, and got him to ostentatiously mark the time as 11.45 p.m. It was barely three o'clock.

At Aberdeen station (here we go again) he checked the departure board. He had an hour to wait before he would be carried back to Seafield but it was a place that he didn't want to go to. He sat in the little bar (a drink was called for after Mrs, sorry, Madame McLintock) and placed her letter in the recess of his bag alongside that of the cloacally obsessed Mr Merryweather, the frenetic Jim, the bereft Mr MacKenzie and the sad Herr Voigts. Slowly he lifted out the final scrappy hope.

"If you really want to make some money and do something" (scrawled out twice before it was properly spelled) "ring me and I will tell you about the Beetls and the things one of them left behind here that kud (sic) be a big thing for you and here. I am not xpensive but need help right now. One of them used to come here and he wrotes (sic) songs and things on the walls. They are worth a bomb and they are OK still. I saw your ad in the *P&J* and am answering it."

105

Donald had forgotten that in a moment of madness he had followed the Vice Chancellor's instructions and advertised in all the regional papers asking for ideas for big tourist ventures. There had been some editorial copy as well and the bulging correspondence file which now covered his office floor had been the result. He realised with as much sadness as shock that all those letters must have been sitting unopened for well over a year.

The smell of sheep hung heavy on the paper and was beginning to infect his hands. The contact phone number seemed vaguely familiar – something he had rung before – and he had a sensation of its being a painful number to remember. He glimpsed someone who looked like Susan as he started on his second drink, and it came to him. The first part was her dialling code and he had rung it once, in an ill-fated attempt to re-open contact. She had not answered.

That proved the letter must be a hoax. Nowhere in that wilderness was there the outstanding relic of an international icon. Nowhere outside America or Liverpool or London could there be such things. It didn't happen. Not even in Glasgow, definitely not in Seafield, and absolutely not there.

He missed, or didn't bother about, the train. He went to another pub, rang a friend he had once been at university with, went to another pub and crashed on a flat floor for the night. It didn't make him feel any better, but it sort of helped him feeling any worse.

Donald got back to Seafield two days later. There was intervening embarrassment about a cash card, and then a cheque and then a lack of money. He spent his Sunday in his office, tapping away at his word processor, which was still regurgitating the things of his it had swallowed. By six there were three sheets of paper ready which had been edited by his skilful hand in a way that made it not absolutely clear if any of the carefully dressed-up projects (Mr Merryweather had become a historian of domestic life with a unique collection, which Heather Pure might well find fascinating) were ones that he would, at this moment in time, recommend except for further study.

Jim was praised as being "visionary but impractical". Donald could not bring himself to describe the shipwreck, but the ferry museum idea was given a cautious welcome, though its drawbacks (no ferries) were weighted against it. Snow ballet and snow opera were described only to be dismissed in the light of reservations from other agencies (he was ashamed of that one). Madame McLintock got the short straw of being impossible to develop, though again the camouflage was good. Her ectoplasmic tearoom was a fine idea.

Only the sheep man (as Donald had become to think of him) stood out as being about as daft as you could get. But even here it was suggested that field research in the first instance would be required to verify a rumour (though not an idle one) that there was a significant historic musical connection in a remote part of Scotland that might be blended with traditional arts (and Heather Pure water) to make something interesting and new. But such field research would have to be considered in terms of a cost–benefit analysis and might not be an immediate priority.

The Vice Chancellor, whilst a wizard of the keyboard and a virtuoso of micro-electronics, preferred papers to be given to him by staff face-to-face, as if in a tutorial. The appointment was already made and Donald knew he could not fail to attend. He was ready, washed and scrubbed, and standing in the anteroom a full minute and a half before Peter pulled open the door, beamed, and gestured him in.

The beaming put Donald on his guard but it was still a shock to find that Peter was not alone. A ruddy, fat but polished man sat in the informal seating area, as Peter liked to call it. Perched on two chairs were men who could only be civil servants. But Peter did not sit down immediately.

"Charlie, this is the young and very promising man you – and your sponsors – have been paying for. It was wise of you to suggest, was it only an hour ago , that we might all meet together before your sponsors landed on these shores. Let me have a word with Donald, though, before we commence."

Peter walked Donald into his second office, the Vice Chancellor needing more than any ordinary man in terms of facilities and space. He closed the door firmly but his mood changed before the two pieces of wood had met.

"I hope to God you are not about to fuck up again. That idiot Charlie MacKellar has jumped us. I told him I was meeting you this morning, prior to our chat on Wednesday, and he turned up bold as brass. He is worried and is piling on the pressure. What have you got "

Donald prepared himself, sometimes, for what was inevitable, but not for what was outrageously unexpected. He burbled, sat down, looked at the floor, and said nothing. He held out his pieces of paper. Peter took them and scanned.

And a remarkable thing happened. He did not scream, or shout, or attack Donald, or throw the china lamp through the window. He read and walked up and down and then looked straight at him.

"Poor stuff, but it will have to do. It has a certain camouflage, which is useful. We will suggest further investigation of Mr Merryweather with a small side bet on the Beatles thing. It will give us a breathing space. For Christ's sake there simply must be better than this in the entire length and breadth of Scotland and you or someone else will have to find it."

Peter pulled the door open and ushered Donald back in. Charlie was standing looking out the window, dismayed to see so much nothing in front of him. Not even a shop – only the sea. No wonder Peter was off his head.

"Charlie, Donald here has a paper I shall pass around. It is being copied now. I suggest we consider how to proceed after we have read it."

And consider they did. Remarkably, Charlie was calm and friendly. They discussed whether Heather Pure would be interested in kitchenware and the development of domestic life. Donald chipped in ideas he had read in the journals about walk-throughs, interactions and experiences. It seemed to occur to nobody that this was all completely irrelevant. It was nowhere near to being a big thing. In fact it was just another little thing, to go with all those other little things that had been tried before.

The e-centre and Jim were quickly rejected. The "Museum of the Ferry Man" was mulled over as being a good idea, but a bit pointless without ferries. Snow opera seemed a drift too far. Madame McLintock they all, fortunately, dismissed. When they got on to the sheep man, it went the same way. Or rather it was going the same way until one of the civil servants spoke for the first time.

"I know where this is," he said. "My wife is from there. I've heard the story before and I certainly thought it was true. It could be fascinating."

"And very profitable," said Charlie, looking up at him. "If it's true and it can be found, then it would be great. It would be what we are looking for."

The mood had changed. If it were true, Heather Pure would have a gold mine and Hi-Fizz would be delighted. Enthusiasm took hold of everyone except Donald. He didn't want to go, not least because that might mean seeing Susan. He didn't believe a word of it. And what would happen when it turned out to be untrue, for the letter was merely the inevitable outcome of advertising in the *Aberdeen Press & Journal*. Thank God he had missed out the *Stornoway Gazette*.

Charlie became adamant. "You must go there now and tell us quickly if it stands up. The drinks people are here on Wednesday, so you have time to get there, do a quick recce and come back." (He didn't, of course, know anything about Scotland's public transport system – he had a chauffeur-driven Jag.) "You can take what you need to help you and I am sure Peter will arrange to meet any costs. If it doesn't work we can say it is still being tried and we will find something else."

The implication was that it would be found without him.

The Vice Chancellor was in his get-of-jail-free mood. He was expansive and generous. He and Charlie went to lunch, but before they departed chits were signed, arrangements for Wednesday were made and Donald was told to get on as quickly as he could with what he needed to do.

Donald came down (in every sense) from the Vice Chancellor's office in a state of shock. It had all gone so much better than it might, but it had still all gone so horribly wrong. It would have been better to end it than to carry on, but he was having to carry on.

Seafield to bugger-all. Taxi (again) to the railhead. Railhead to Glasgow, as before – change in Edinburgh. Glasgow to Inverness, through the heart of Scotland though the train rattled and shook and the buffet car was closed at Aviemore. Inverness in the evening, and the last train to Ultima Thule caught by the skin of his teeth. A moorland station with no taxis, but there was a phone. A hotel somewhere close by.

But the journey was worse than that, because while leaving his flat he tripped over the mat and found a letter. He kept on reading it as the rails clicked past. It was true. She knew it was. There was a big thing. And she had found it.

15. IMAGINE

Well spotted. There were indeed seven projects on Donald's list, but he has only written up six of them for the Vice Chancellor, for Charlie and (ultimately) for Hiram. In fact he never got to see the seventh, even though it was the best project of all and just what Scotland needs. That is also why it would never have attracted Hi-Fizz or Heather Pure.

Amongst all the millennium-funded, architect-designed, "This will make all the difference to the community", "Scotland is once again in the forefront of visitor attractions", "If only we can get the money together, we'll show them" experiences, theme parks, fun rides and domes there are some things that are about more than the 21st century and its relentless desire for modernity.

These are the things that try and remind us who we are and where we came from. Which celebrate what we have done, and suggest to us what we can do. Things like museums, presided over by men and women with a passion for history (like Donald) and prepared to take the long view. To use time to reflect on time. To collect and to preserve and to research and to interpret, even if no one comes to see what has been collected, preserved, researched and interpreted.

Mr Merryweather, Mr MacKenzie and Madame McLintock had glimpsed that this was the real task, the real direction in which their enthusiasms should be channelled. But instead of using time to reflect on time, they had gone for the quick idea, for the crudely burnished segment of the whole which is usually the only way to attract support. And that was their downfall.

Donald's seventh project lay in the foothills of the Highlands, in a place which had nurtured humankind for millennia. It was surrounded by burial kists, by cup and ring marks, by rock carvings, by scripts chiselled into boulders. It was in sight of a hill where there was a fort older than Scottish or Gaelic speech, and on which the rulers of a savage kingdom made their vows and slaughtered to protect their people.

From Donald's seventh project, sitting in the little glass-walled cafeteria, one could see the sparkling lochs that led to the sea and to the islands. Turning one's head, one could stare down upon a ring of standing stones, though no one knew its builders and their purpose.

For years a few people who cared about this landscape and what it meant had built up a business, which lurched from financial crisis to financial crisis and which survived only on imagination and hard work. Officials came and visited and sometimes a way was found of shoehorning the passion, dedication and care into the narrow constricting slipper of application forms and funding regulations.

Although visitors came and fell in love with the place and the idea of the place, without the money to advertise, without the help of the SVA ("We don't promote individual projects below a certain size, I am sorry") without the support – in every sense – of the local council ("No road signs giving directions to single unapproved centres can be authorised under the Planning (Scotland) Act 1973, you know – you'll have to take it down") and without a government that wanted its people to know about the country they owned and was prepared to do something rather than just talk – without all of these whatever future there was got darker and more threadbare each year.

You can only put so much effort in, before stopping becomes easier than going on. By the time that Donald had seen the letter (one of thousands they had written over the years, and sent in any direction that might help) the little cafeteria was closed, the small exhibition space left to gather dust and the car park overgrown with willowherb. And when Donald rang to arrange a visit, the phone was answered only by a machine, which

112

said that the centre had been forced to shut the preceding October. Thank you for calling. Beep.

Hi-Fizz would never have bought it, anyway. Not without installing a ride, building a fake underground chamber, and arranging simulated human sacrifices at 12, 2 and 4 (in season). And if they had done that, where would the time have been to collect, preserve, research and interpret. Where would the space be for the wind to blow through the marsh grass? Where would the boulder be, marked with ogham script, behind which a visitor could look for shelter from the rain? And where would the sense of history be, and of our place in it – our place in this age-old, strange, long-civilised country which we do not know and about which we are discovering less and less?

16. WE CAN WORK IT OUT

Susan didn't sleep much that night. The sun, which hardly set, shone through the thin curtains and seemed to highlight what was on the wall. By the time she decided to get up the drawings appeared bigger and louder than they had been the night before, when Iain had gawped and then sat down on the bed.

But strangely she also felt that they were a little further away than they had been last night. The issue of their future was already moving towards some form of conclusion, whatever that was.

Today, she knew, she would have to make decisions. It could not be covered up because somebody else knew and in any case there was no way she could even start to stick all the pieces of paper together again so that nothing showed.

Iain's "day or two" would, she thought, be the maximum. If one person knew, even Iain, then the whole world was in the process of knowing and the whole world would therefore turn to her little cottage, above the fence, and start to intrude. She might persuade herself to wait for that, on the very off chance that it would not happen, but she would still be terrified.

This would not only change what was around her, it would change her. And despite the manifest ways in which she longed for change, she did not want it, or she did not want it yet.

Showering and dressing was automatic, though the shower was the plasticky, bought for a holiday home, dribble on your head when you are in the bath, type of thing and she much preferred the torrent type that gave you a headache if you stood under it for too long but certainly woke you up. Then she ambled down to the office, sorted through the mail (two letters of complaint from members who were getting nothing for their money, three circulars from the SVA with lots of flow charts and digital coding instructions on them and some enquiries including one from a woman in Brighton and Hove who wanted to know about polar bears), and having killed time by re-stacking the leaflets and rearranging the book shelves (yet again) she ambled up to the bar when she thought there would be someone to talk to over an early lunch.

Iain was nowhere to be seen, but Ewan the barman had an envelope for her. It contained a single piece of paper which simply said "£55,000". She sat down on her own, as the place was empty, had her usual lunchtime mineral water, and thought.

She would have carried on thinking for quite a while had the bar door not opened and had Donald Keays not walked in and peered around, looking for someone to talk to about a room.

Then he gulped, stared goggle-eyed and dropped his bag which proceeded to vomit half its contents on the floor. She on the other hand (she is more composed and a bit more of an actor) fought down her panic, smiled enigmatically and raised her glass.

She had to buy him a drink, of course (after she had retrieved his bits and pieces, including a can of deodorant which had rolled under the pool table), because he was incapable of much except opening and closing his mouth and saying things like "How are you " and "I got your letter" and – for he was an honest man, though usually because most of the time he hadn't the courage to be anything else – "I am here to see it, but there's a problem".

Susan had known as soon as she had seen him that there was a problem. Iain knowing was one thing that would lead to consequences. Donald knowing was quite another, for the consequences that would lead to were, literally, incalculable, though the level of mathematical imagination which would be required to calculate them (there are lots and lots of zeros) increased exponentially as Donald managed to tell his story.

She filtered out the bits about Mr Merryweather and Mr MacKenzie and Madame McLintock (and even the bit that Donald told her about the place he hadn't put in his report) though she knew she wanted to hear them later and especially in the way he told them. She bored down into the detail and the detail was very worrying. Not only Donald knew. The Vice Chancellor knew, the SVA knew and even the Scottish Executive knew, if by "knowing" you mean that the civil servants possessed a nugget of information. There was a bit of comfort (though it was foolish) in that the story was merely a possibility, a rumour, a speculation. Yet speculation does well enough for many people. Seeing it in print only confirms it, even if it's not as much as half true.

They dispensed with the thought of lunch and she took him back to the office (with raised eyebrows from Mary, who had heard about him many times before) and then they went for a walk on the beach and eventually held hands. She even kissed him, as she knew she would.

They went back to the house and she showed it to him – though she kept on the other side of the bed because she knew him well and what he would be thinking she might want. And then they sat down again by the kitchen table and started to talk about what to do.

Segment the problem. Susan knew that if she just allowed all this to happen she would be swept along in it until it dropped her on a stony emotional shore a week, a month, a year from now. Donald would be safe, of course,

116

even if he was unhappy, and they both knew that what he was doing now was so irrelevant that being safe was irrelevant too – perhaps it made it worse. She might make a lot of money, but that would just be another reason for guilt.

But if she stood up against it, and had it her way then something precious would be destroyed for ever, because the genie and the genius couldn't go back in the bottle and there was no way that it could only be hidden. It would have to be destroyed, to go, to disappear, to be ground down into dust and scattered to the winds. It must cease to be. The rumour of it would go on, of course, and people would talk about it on winter nights in the pub and how John Lennon did leave something there, yet it would never be found. Why, it hadn't been found even by the girl who had bought the house.

Around them darkness came. They carried on talking. What would happen to them, they wondered If Heather Pure wanted research done – and they would – they would bring in experts, but there would be a place (the Vice Chancellor would see to that) for the University of Seafield, Department of Applied Tourism. Donald would come back and forward but she would have gone, unable to accept the notoriety, not willing to be the catalyst. He would be miserable. He would get over it. Perhaps she would too.

She had no idea what would happen to her, but down that route she saw a distinguished spinsterhood with occasional lovers. It was another role she had wondered about playing.

They dipped backwards and forwards, peering at the problem, trying to see another way. They almost believed they could turn the clock back, and Donald would pretend that there was nothing, and she would pretend that she did not know and try to persuade Iain. They would go back to their old lives and find a better way forward together, separately, somewhere, somehow.

117

He would go and tell the Vice Chancellor that it was there, but it was nothing. He would disappear for a while, taking the sheep man's note with him. Donald could have a breakdown, an alcoholic collapse (though actually he didn't drink nearly enough for that), an early midlife crisis, and that would explain everything. But if the mysterious sheep man knew, it occurred to both of them at the same time, then who else did And who was the sheep man anyway

It came to that moment when there was no choice at all. They moved forward or they fell backward – whatever would happen, would happen. Perhaps even a bit of both. And they would have stayed like that, and wanted to stay like that, if the phone had not rung and if it had not been Iain.

"We have a problem. You had better come down to the bar, but come to the kitchen door."

She took Donald with her as Iain needed to know that problem too. Iain opened the kitchen door and did not seem fazed by the presence of a person he had never met in his life before, even though the person seemed to be holding Susan's hand as if it had always been part of him.

"I presume I can talk. Anyway, you need to know. Out there in the bar is a journalist from the *Daily Record* and he knows about the house. Or rather he thinks he knows about the house. An anonymous tip-off, he says, and he wants to know where it is. I have got Calum and the others stalling him with drink, but I suspect he can drink them under the table. We need a decision and we need it fast."

If it had been possible to do a slow slide under the metal-topped kitchen counter and curl up with her hands over her head, Susan would have done so. She envied those who could. But instead, with a gulp, she told him Donald's story – Donald chipped in with the irrelevancies – and they worked out that it was not the sheep man – Iain could put a name to him, but he was dead (Donald was slow in

118

attending to his correspondence). So it was probably Charlie or the civil servant, keen for notoriety, to make a bob or two, to matter in the story. Or the Vice Chancellor, who was always on the make and who made his own stories.

Iain kept checking the bar, but within an hour Calum, Allan and the boys were uproarious and the *Record* journalist was just listening. He had booked a room, and wasn't going anywhere tonight. Tomorrow he would be better armed for another day.

Moments of crisis have a lot of night talking in them. No wonder the players get exhausted and irrational and start to fray at the edges. None the less Iain and Susan and Donald talked around and inside and over the problem until a glimmer of light came from the greasy window and illuminated a bag of tools lying on the floor. Of course, under the Health and Safety Acts it shouldn't have been there.

It was Iain who saw it first. Susan later thought she might have but she was some seconds behind him.

"We can't just take it all down," he said.

And then he said, "Why not Why not take it all down No one would believe that it has been removed, because no one really knows except us that it exists. If they come to find it, well they already think we are all daft here. They will go away cursing us and their wasted effort and the wild goose chase and that will be the end of it. We will take it down as if it never was. But we will keep it safe, because we owe it to more than us to allow others to have the choice. You" – and he swept Susan and Donald up together in one gesture – "will keep it safe. That will be your job."

Donald thought Iain had gone mad. He wondered about rising from the table so that he could put himself at a distance from the sharp knives. But Susan grasped the answer that Iain was offering, though she also saw the problems.

"How can we take a house down How can we do it when there is a journalist here, and no doubt more to come How can we do it when Donald has to go back and tell the truth, and he has to go back tomorrow "

"Trust me," said Iain. "I'm a builder. Most builders aren't very good at putting things up, but they are dab hands at knocking things down. I think I can see how to do it, but we need to work out how to get it right."

They should have gone home to their beds, but Susan had no bed she now wanted to sleep in and she didn't want to sleep. So Iain got paper and pencil and they worked out a way of making a house on a hill above a fence disappear as if by magic. And they worked out how to keep it safe and to make it something even better which held its mystery inside for them to see if they wished. And they worked out how to keep the world at bay while they did it in a twinkling of an eye.

It would need help, determination, guile, courage and even a little bit of luck. What it didn't need was what it was about to get, which was another dose of reality, in the shape of the Vice Chancellor.

17. DO YOU WANT TO KNOW A SECRET?

Scottish hotels (and their kitchens) are as varied as the country itself.

The good ones don't kowtow to corporate reality. They have long since seen through the views of interfering busybodies in organisations which proscribe what valances, kettles, TVs, duvets, curtains, towels and bathrobes are required to move from grade to grade in their dull catalogues. Hotels like the Ceilidh Place in Ullapool, where Jean Urquhart knows more about life than any SVA inspector, has even the courage to keep a bookshop where people with ideas meet from time to time to talk about them – a dangerous thing in Scotland, so it has to be done in secret.

Further north, on that coast we are learning about, there is another bookshop. It is kept by two men who have also made it a restaurant. They are wonderful people because they also have ideas and curiosity and they have come through hell to do what they want with and for each other. Sydney Smith's idea of heaven was "eating pâté de foie gras to the sound of trumpets". He would have found it even more heavenly in a bookshop.

Far out to sea on a flat lump of land there is another hotel, which couldn't be more different. Its new owners have ruined the Creagorry, for it used to be shabby and unpretentious with one of the most famous bars in Scotland and now it is just tarty and like everywhere else. It has been in two novels already – Fionn MacColla's and Neil Gunn's – and now it is in a third. It used to sell, they said, more whisky than any other establishment in urope. To just 2000 people!

On another island there is the Lochmaddy Hotel. It is very like the bar in which Susan was drinking when Donald opened the door. It has a slot machine and beer-stained tables and the place *changes hands with local-gossip-grabbing regularity and seems to decline further each time.*

Low life or luxury – take your choice. The Caley Palace in Gatehouse of Fleet, which is like the set for Brideshead Revisited *and which just errs on the side of down-market. The Popinjay at Rosebank, horribly full of car salesmen from Glasgow, with their BMWs parked outside and who think they are making it in the world. The Caledonian in dinburgh, where Sean Connery stays when he is in town, in a film-star-like suite complete with bowls of fruit and the glimpse of a ruffled bed through the lounge door. The Pennan Inn, a wave flick away from the shore, whose rooms are crowded and whose ceilings are low. The Marine Highland, where you lie in bed at night and hear the planes landing at Prestwick. The Alexandra in Fort William, whose antiquated heating pipes are red hot on snow-covered mornings. The Haws Inn under the bridge, the Castlebay above the ferry, the shell of* The Scotsman, *where they used to do important things, The Kings Arms in Melrose (robbed from Kissling), the Open Arms at Direlton and its talking wood, The Selkirk Arms in Kirkcudbright, innumerable Royals, Stations (including the one with grumpy staff in Inverness but from which you can hear the trains arrive and leave), South Beaches, North Beaches, and even the odd (still) Imperial.*

Hotels in every corner of our land, with sticky carpets or inches-deep shagpile, with silver service or microwave meals. Through whose greasy kitchen windows comes the smell of deep fat and frying and the clattering shouts of people trying to make their living.

It is not whether they are good or bad that makes the real difference. There is more hope in honest error, as Rennie Mackintosh said, than in the icy perfection of the mere stylist. It is whether they are run with passion and imagination and whether those who run them welcome the passer-by, or are too busy to see him (or her). Who want to do what they do, even if few come. And who, having done it, believe they have done it well.

18. HELP!

Some say that there are three personages whose switchboards can find anyone in the world at a moment's notice: the Queen, the Prime Minister and the President of the United States. One suspects that the Pope and the Dalai Lama might also be in this category, though with divine rather than technological intervention. However, the Vice Chancellor liked to think that he was at least somewhere in touching distance of this premier league of busybodies, for the Vice Chancellor was legendary for being able to contact, as he called them, "colleagues". The Professor of Meteorology, whose discipline had existed before the Vice Chancellor's time but was now in avalanche-like decline in status and funding, had once been located in an observation station on K2. But to Peter that was small beer.

He could find people in airports, in supermarkets, on the Amazon, in bed with other people whom they thought nobody knew about, and sometimes he could find them when they themselves believed they were lost. The messages he had to impart on these occasions were not tremendously important but the very act of contact impressed on the contactee who they were dealing with, and reinforced the contactor's already monumental sense of self-importance.

It was thus not beyond him to have planted a bug on Donald so that he could track his movements by geostationary satellite as he hurtled north. But because Peter and Charlie needed to square up at lunch, he had not thought of doing such a thing until it was too late and Donald had gone.

The lunch had been important. Nothing but pleasantries and gossip were exchanged, but these two men did not need conversation to measure what was happening. Peter knew Charlie was in trouble. Charlie knew Peter's career was on the line. If they could help each other this time, despite their cordial dislike, then there would be no debts outstanding and they might be more effective working together than working apart. If they could not, then one of them would find a way to survive by sacrificing the other.

But both glimpsed that it was downhill from then on if they made a mistake or weakened. It was the Reichenbach falls. Not that it made a long-term difference. They also knew that even if they survived on this knife-edge, then they survived only for the inevitable next battle and for the one (the next or the next or the next) that they must eventually lose. Perhaps it was only a case of "Not yet, oh Lord, not yet".

Yet they lived for this. For winning, not losing. For prestige and power and all the other things that people fool themselves with even when they think they are long past the ability to be tempted by any whiff of such folly.

The Vice Chancellor fretted a little that evening, with his soon-to-be fourth wife. She thought it might be her, so she diverted him. He came back from the diversion refreshed and clearer-headed. She thought he was clear-headed for her and she was therefore surprised to see him rise, put on his more casual clothes – the ones he wore for being thirty-something again – and call for his driver. Surprised too because it was the middle of the night.

His driver – one of a team, such were the demands upon them – was not surprised. He knew that he wouldn't get through a week of nights without a summons at some stage and as the money was good (paid from a special account donated by a sympathetic widow in Arkansas), he did what he was asked and only told his mates about it.

Within half an hour they were on the road. If you want the directions, you shall have them. Slightly north and then west, past the sleeping city of Perth (Scotland does its cities on rivers well: Dumfries, Inverness, Perth, dream places all) and then north again, racing by mountains and sweeping over rivers with powerful headlights slashing the dark. Over the biggest river, over the fault line and then eventually north-west into a landscape of quiet and heather, where the few remaining ptarmigan rose each dawn. Finally, as Peter dozed with half an eye open, the car breasted a hill and there was the huge ocean, stretching to the frozen pole.

Highland hotels do not open early. There is little passing breakfast trade and even if there was, most still wouldn't open in time. So Iain was surprised to hear a banging at his door barely an hour after Donald and Susan had left and more surprised still to see in front of him a tall, elegant, casually well dressed man and behind him a chauffeur-driven car.

Coffee was asked for, and provided. A mobile phone (this was one of the small oases of signal on the whole journey) was shouted into as Peter instructed his very early-rising secretary about changes in the day's routine. A room to wash and change was requested and paid for at more than the going rate. Indications were given that it might be required for the night as well. The chauffeur was sent to a bed and breakfast. And then a question was asked.

"Have you, by any chance, seen a young man round here called Donald Keays "

Iain had guessed it at once, but he was not giving up his plan without a fight.

"What would he be like "

"Like someone who doesn't come from here and who is looking for something. You have seen him"

"I might be able to find him. Who shall I say wants to see him"

"Tell him that his Vice Chancellor is here to help him."

Iain left Donald and Susan for a few hours and then – making sure that he was not observed, though he felt that the Vice Chancellor could probably observe everything – he made his way to the house above the fence.

They were bleary-eyed, but up and drinking yet more tea at the kitchen table.

"Another problem, I am afraid. Your Vice Chancellor is here. He wants you but he doesn't know where you are. I think you will have to see him."

After a period of regular shocks, applied out of the blue, new ones either freak us out, or are quietly absorbed with an anaesthetised shrug. Donald got freaked out – Susan absorbed. She calmed him down again and then they made some more plans and revised those that they had already put in place.

Part I (revised) required a clean shirt for Donald, which was fortunately in his still sea-water-damp bag along with socks, underwear, assorted toiletries – some of which had leaked over the years – a crumpled jacket, two books and in the lining an old half-packet of biscuits. The biscuits were discarded.

Part II (revised) needed Donald to tell the Vice Chancellor nearly everything – the *Record* journalist, the leak, the local rumours that Iain had told Susan, and the fact that the house existed and he was trying to get a look at it. But he was not – absolutely not – to tell the Vice Chancellor where the house was or that he knew the person in it. If pressed (and he would be), he was to say that it was outside the village and that he was talking to someone who knew someone who had a key or a secret tunnel or something. He was to imply shutters and barbed wire, and he might, if necessary, lean on the likely tactics of the Gaelic mafia, well known around these parts, who if they got a hint of curiosity about the place would explain very slowly in accented English the wrong way to get anywhere, suggest routes which led through bogs and areas laden with ferocious midges, might well block progress along single-track roads by driving ancient tractors very slowly and who would call on the traditions of the Sabbath to make certain that everything happened in geological time. Talking of minefields was a last resort but was allowed.

He was unlikely to make the Vice Chancellor go away. But he might pause for reinforcements.

Part III (original but now slightly revised) needed to go into effect that day, and be ready for that night. The forecast was for cloud but no rain, with the occasional shaft of moonlight. People were to be recruited and sworn to silence, tools borrowed or stolen, the quietest lorries rounded up, turf found and cut, a hiding place secured, the band booked and a little bottle sought from a man who lived up a glen underneath the big hill.

Part IV (original) would wait a bit longer until things had settled down. There was a place for it, on the edge of the village, where the bay curved into the land. Much needed to be prepared.

So they started. Donald washed and changed and Susan tightened his tie and he walked out of the back door with Iain, away from the fence, then back down towards the village and the hotel. It was a straight amble into the lounge where the Vice Chancellor was barking on his phone. Iain left them to it, but propped open the serving hatch so that he could hear what was being said.

Perhaps the sea air, or his tiredness, had transformed him, if only temporarily. Donald played his part like a

127

trouper. Even Iain got worried about going anywhere near this mythical house, which seemed to combine Gormenghast with Frankenstein's castle and be guarded not merely by Dracula but by the Four Horsemen of the Apocalypse as well, albeit riding Clydesdales or ancient Fordsons. Reinforcements were being discussed when Iain heard a rapping at the reception desk and slipped away.

His receptionists came and went, and this summer's one was an Australian, bright of feature, buxom, still tanned, the toast of the boys in the bar, absolutely here today and completely gone tomorrow. As he reached the office she was trying to make sense of the requirements of an American, a bluff Glaswegian and a silent little man who must be a civil servant. They seemed to want, simultaneously, en suite facilities, an early lunch, a map of the area, a b&b for a chauffeur and stories about John Lennon. The latter was the problem, not least because the *Daily Record* journalist was standing open-mouthed at the bottom of the stairs.

His mouth opened even wider when the Vice Chancellor of Seafield University, dressed for casual city life, emerged from another room.

"Charlie, how nice to see you – and so soon. I had wondered when you would turn up. Please introduce me to your American friend, though I suspect he must be Hiram Heidelberg, the President of Hi-Fizz and – if the papers are to be believed – the new owner of Heather Pure." He ignored the civil servant. They came and went even though they were ultimately in charge.

Introductions were made and the Vice Chancellor called for coffee, installed them in the lounge and started to talk.

"I quite understand your desire to see what may be here as soon as possible. There are problems, but they can be overcome. I can confirm that the story is true. What we must decide first is that if – and it is now a more likely if – this remarkable thing can be obtained, on what terms we are all going to obtain it.

"You, Mr Heidelberg – Hiram, of course – will need to make the investment. I suspect we can obtain the thing very cheaply, even *in situ*. A maximum of a hundred thousand dollars, which you have probably either got on you or can get with the sweep of a card. Good. Naturally much more will be needed later.

"Charlie, you will want to be able to announce this once it is secure and to commit the SVA to a partnership – a long-standing partnership – with Heather Pure to ensure sensitive, environmentally friendly, serious and profitable exploitation, of everything including the local tourist infrastructure. The Minister will be delighted – it is all really just in time, isn't it

"For my part, my colleague here and I only exist to serve. We will be very pleased to be retained as independent academics to advise on the development, to research it and to publish on it. A department that could do that will need to be of suitable size and stature but I am sure you would want nothing else. We will need, for a start, a world-renowned Lennon expert. Seafield is the right, indeed, the only place for such a man, I am sure. The Executive" – he nodded at the civil servant who had not even started to take notes – "will confirm that too, I suspect.

"Now" – and even Charlie was still silent – "we must marshal our forces. Donald is going back out to locate the building, to recce the problems and to report in detail. We will spend the afternoon walking and talking and working out the details of the deal. Tonight I will buy you the best dinner that can be had hereabouts and I will call in additional help, with your permission, if really needed. Tomorrow we should be in position."

There wasn't much left for anyone else to say. Hiram said lots of things at great length but he was in agreement and money was no object. His second wife's third son, who was giving them trouble, was a Beatles fan and this would help. He could not afford another divorce at the moment and, gee, he liked Scotland. This would make a buck.

Charlie knew he had lost, but in losing had been given – as he usually was – a lifeline that would keep him going, ensure that the right people continued to think moderately well of him and might still use his fixing abilities.

The civil servant was wondering when he could write all this down, and make it real.

The *Daily Record* journalist, who had sat in the corner and listened, thought about filing his copy until he looked at Charlie and Peter and realised that until they were ready, it wouldn't get printed. Charlie said he would talk to his editor. Peter would too. An exclusive was promised with his byline. A book deal was hinted at. An evening of drinking was dangled before him. And expenses.

Only Donald remained troubled. The plan would need another revision to take account of not just eagle-eyed Peter, but ferret-eyed Charlie as well. And the plan was so unlikely, so magical, so fey in every description that anything could go wrong, and these people could find themselves in charge yet again. In charge and knowing that Donald and Iain and Susan had lied to them. These people didn't forgive – they were the establishment mafia that left the Gaelic one looking like boy scouts.

"A word of warning, Donald, if I may," interrupted the Vice Chancellor, as if reading his thoughts. Leading him into the corridor, he poked a finger at his chest and said, "I won't track your movements because I know you can't get away. But if you do something silly then there won't be a Donald to come back to Seafield and all that you might have there. I am sure you understand. And your friends – if you have any – will find out about life too."

"Fucking right," said Charlie, who had followed.

"See you soon, Donald," said Peter. "Shall we say seven o'clock For dinner " He was dismissed.

"And now, perhaps, a dram if you would like one, Hiram " said Peter, sweeping back into the lounge. "A dram being what we Scots call a measure – a generous measure – of our best malt whisky."

Iain would have brought it in without being properly asked (which would have given him away) so riveting was the scene that was being played out, and so commanding was the Vice Chancellor. But Iain was off organising the night's events, so they spent some time trying to be relaxed with each other until the Australian girl was found and drinks were ordered. Peter eyed her up as she delivered the tray. There might be some compensations in this place, after all, he thought, apart from the lack of power and money. And the miles and miles of bugger-all.

19. ALL YOU NEED IS LOVE

How do we understand this world of ours, this place where we were born, or grew up, or chose to be, or found ourself in (it doesn't matter)? How do we understand ourselves in that place and time? How do we make that understanding create our future?

As we grew in money and choices, we somehow became diminished, and we knew it. We thought we owned it all and could make it better, but really we were passing it by. We seem – most of us – to have stopped telling ourselves the stories that explain it all: indeed we stopped explaining. But stories are what our ancestors needed to make sense of the things that happened to them and where they happened.

The selkies called and took people away and they drowned, yet they lived in the memories and happiness of those who were left behind. They were living and loving under the sea.

True Thomas lay on Huntley bank, but he died too and yet his memory went on and he was rhyming still. And even at the Sheiling of the One Night, those who had wandered too far and had terrible things happen to them, even they were saved for ever (despite their folly) by the man who came back with an awful secret he could not speak of, even in daylight.

Understanding this is not fun. We don't have to do it. But if we don't do it, we are less than we can be. If we don't do it then we are divorced, separated, cut off from the river that runs through us and in which we can cool our ardours, slake our thirsts, float when we need support, emerging from it clean and pure. We are merely human.

And what has this to do with Donald and Susan? verything – for now is their chance to participate in myth. The little people will come and remove their problem though it will remain in their keeping for ever. They will be alive at last and know what it is to live.

The little people had pickaxes and hammers and at least one of them had a pronounced problem with bad breath. Some had secrets they didn't want anyone to know and thought they had done awful things. They were hiders from reality, makers of tall tales, cheaters on their wives, betrayers of their children, smokers, drinkers, onanists – all those things and more.

But they were also makers of legends. For this is a moment when the land and the people are one, and when the love of the land and the love that it gives is a force as great as the love between Donald and Susan.

Countries change. The conversation of the people and the earth goes on for ever.

20. A HARD DAY'S NIGHT

Donald went back up the hill but found the little house empty, which was a disappointment. He settled down on the settee in what used to be called the parlour and went to sleep.

Susan and Iain, meanwhile, were busy. People were called and asked to come to the village hall. Before they came they were told nothing except that they were needed like they had never been needed before. And they were told in terms that demanded silence.

Susan had packed what little she wanted to keep and had gone back to work, ostensibly because that was what would look right, but actually to search the Net for some information on cutting up, removing, keeping safe and then restoring. She eventually found it, with profound thanks to the geek who had put it all there. Iain had also asked her to book the band, and she eventually found the mover and shaker who was doing nothing that night and was available, though he was surprised to be asked. For a gig only, of course. He was told nothing else. But it was to be a long gig.

Iain meanwhile had driven a couple of miles out of the village and had walked over a little bridge to a ramshackle cottage beside a burn. He was admitted by an old man and he took tea. They talked in Gaelic about fishing, about the salmon rising, about seaweed and its miraculous properties on potatoes, though the old man looked too frail to plant potatoes or collect seaweed. Iain was offered something without asking for it, and of course he took the bottle, wrapped in a brown paper bag that once contained morning rolls. After a decent time he left with a grave "thank you". He re-crossed the little stream and returned to the hotel where he put the bottle in his old safe.

The Vice Chancellor and Charlie had gone for a gentle walk. They were at the pier when Iain drove past, peering at boats like tourists. Hiram was in his room trying to call long-distance, arguing with his wife. The civil servant had gone hiking (they always do). The journalist was drinking (they always do).

The Australian had not yet had a pass made at her by Peter, but she was happily expecting it. She passed on the request for dinner in a quiet room, though it would be quiet anyway as they were the only guests apart from the journalist, and for local ingredients – venison and salmon had been suggested. Certain red wines had been asked for which Iain hadn't got but would pretend he had. Above all there was to be privacy.

"There will be a dance tonight," Iain then told her. "If Ewan needs help in the bar – and he will – you can give it to him. I will serve dinner and my wife will cook it."

There is a quiet hour in any hotel before dinner. In good hotels it is the time to sit with a drink, properly dressed, and anticipate. In bad hotels one tries to do the same, but fails. In countries where they know how to live, one walks the square, chooses a restaurant, goes to another bar to sit on the veranda, and holds the hand of one's lover in the warm still evening air while watching the world go by.

By eight o'clock, the appointed time, everything was ready. The meal was almost cooked, the local salmon laid onto plates, the venison bubbling in dark chocolate (she was a sophisticate, was Iain's wife) and the cranachan chilling in the fridge. The wines were decanted, the best glass and silver was on the table and even some flowers. Dinner for

135

four (the *Record* journalist had had a burger) was prepared. Iain knew Donald would be too late to eat it.

Meanwhile there were people arriving at the hall. Iain started there, talking to each one, giving them their jobs, not explaining the whole thing, but telling them that this was their life's work, their victory, their Bannockburn, the night they would remember for ever, doing something remarkable, and only be able to talk to one another about it, and that not often. The plan was agreed with barely a dissension – though the joiner was worried about saving the rotten wood – and the men who had the task of cutting the blocks from the wall got a special briefing from Susan, with printouts and diagrams and much discussion of plaster.

Could they do it In rather less than twelve hours – the less the better He didn't know. But he hoped.

He was back at the hotel in time to serve the venison. The Australian had filled in for him up until that time, and that was distraction enough for Peter. Secret favours, sweet and precious, were already beginning to flow. Iain took over and the Australian went to the bar where Peter said he would join her later. Iain flourished the wines and flattered the guests but he volunteered only the smallest pieces of information, and he listened behind the door as Charlie and Peter got mildly drunk with an easily susceptible Hiram.

The band arrived to a flurry of bemused disbelief from the pub's usual clientele. Iain was knowledgeable about music and these were not the musicians most of his friends (they are all friends in a bar) would have thought he would choose. No one within fifty miles chose them and certainly not twice. "The Black Night Deaths Head Motorcycle Ceilidh Band" were an interesting, not to say unique, fusion of gothic, hard rock and Scottish traditional. "Fusion", though, was not a word that appealed to them. Their volume was more reminiscent of fission, the type that was the destroyer of worlds.

136

Iain took their leader aside.

"Two hundred and fifty quid for eight hours. Then if I need you, fifty quid an hour thereafter. I tell you when to stop playing. And, of course, all the drink you can take."

This was a Las Vegas-style gig for the band. More – it was Caesar's Palace and Madison Square Gardens all rolled into one. Their time had come. Money was irrelevant (though they had never before been offered any to play). What was spectacular was that they had been offered all they could drink, because no one could ever have imagined such a quantity. There was not enough strong cider and blackcurrant in the world, they thought, to underwrite such an offer.

"Done."

But Iain also told them not to start until he was ready. They trooped to the bar, wide-eyed.

Two things remained to be put in place. Susan had wakened Donald earlier and he had rung the Vice Chancellor. He was making progress and would be back at nine. He would join the dinner for coffee and liqueurs. He would help them to make plans.

Iain rang the foreman appointed for the evening. He knew more than most, in every sense. "We start at ten. On the dot. First crew to take it apart inside without anyone seeing anything. We do the outside when that is done. The boys can start cutting the turf at the old fank now."

Donald arrived bang on nine but even he had not been told everything. Otherwise he would not have come.

Peter was by now reciting poetry, to impress not Hiram (who was almost asleep) or Charlie (who was almost drunk) but the Australian who was hovering at his end of the table, leaning deliberately backward to allow Peter to see that her blouse and her skirt did not meet in the middle. And that she had a jewel just where it should be. Of course, he had noticed both hours before.

137

Coffee was served and then Iain appeared with a flourish. He had changed into tartan trews and was carrying a tray loaded with bottles.

"Gentlemen," he intoned. Peter was briefly annoyed – this would slow down progress towards the seduction. "Gentlemen, there is a tradition in this part of the Highlands that visitors are offered the best we have, and the best we have here is whisky. If you will permit me, I shall give you something you will never have again."

Peter and Charlie liked to be called "gentlemen" by distinguished servants. It brought back to them the deference and recognition they thought was their due. They were sentimental about tradition too, as most people are whose actions destroy it. They accepted with a suffusion of self-satisfied pleasure, and Iain began his lecture.

It was a brief lecture because it knew precisely where it was going. Small glasses were laid, and filled, and sipped, and then drunk. Stories – often untrue stories – were told of distilleries old and new and the miraculous powers of the drink, of which James Hogg, our wonderful shepherd (wonderful not least because he refused an invitation to the coronation of George IV in order not to miss the annual St Boswells market) said that if its true nature were known, doctors and dying would go out of business. The summation came. Iain produced the undistinguished bottle which had lain in his safe for only a few hours.

"This," he said, "is the best. The absolute best and you cannot buy it." Hiram was shocked to the core by that. It was the first thing he had ever seen which he could not buy.

"It is made by one man whose father and grandfather and grandfathers to the many generations knew its secret. And only them. Not one in a million people in the world will ever taste it. But when they do they know that there is nothing better."

138

From the sideboard he produced five exquisite glasses, rimmed with an old gold that had faded but not lost its quiet lustre. He poured a full measure into each of them and handed them over, one by one. They did not drink until all of them held the glasses in their hands, and until they had examined its colour and appreciated its nose.

Then gravely and formally he said – in a commanding whisper – "Take off your dram", and although they did not all understand him, each of them supped the contents in a single motion.

The effect was as it always was when drinking Old Donald's moonshine, particularly on top of an evening's libations. There was a look of pleasure, followed by a look of horror, followed by a gasping breath, and then silence. They did not sleep, they just sat with their brains and bodies switched off and divorced from one another. They were corpses frozen in time. Fortunately the glasses were always laid down first, even the cheap ones.

Right, thought Iain. That gives us, by my experience and the reckoning of the many generations who afterwards wished they were dead, twelve hours, give or take about thirty minutes. All we need now is the noise from the band.

The Dark Night Deaths Head Motorcycle Ceilidh Band were still enjoying – such an inadequate word – the best night of their lives, as it involved drinking a bar dry at no cost to anyone but the landlord. They had to be corralled, cajoled and then driven towards the stage, but eventually they tuned up and the decibels started. The earth moved. It moved again. It could not get comfortable. Sheep shivered, old people on neighbouring islands turned down their hearing aids (but they could still feel it) and the fish migrated rapidly in shoals from any nearby shore.

The band played on.

Thirty minutes to go, thought Iain, as he let himself out the kitchen door. The bar should be empty or stunned within about half an hour, so it was safe to let the boys get going on time. No one would believe anything they saw for several hours.

What would they have seen In the gloaming ten men in dark clothes arriving at the house above the fence. They are let in by Susan, who has piles of clothes and boxes of things sitting in the hall. They are whisked away to a waiting van.

The furniture goes. It is carried onto a blacked-out lorry. It is driven away.

Then they start at the top, taking down the attic floor, stripping the walls in as much silence as they can, but with speed. You have never seen builders working like this. It is unique. The electrician disconnects the house from the mains (they are leaving the cable from the road – too difficult) and unwires it, pulling it out line by line. The telephone wires go too (they have a telephone man, who doubles as a driver).

The plumber unplumbs, careful to cut off the mains, and he blocks the pipe to the septic tank. They will take the risk of leaving things that are not visible.

Joiners remove skirting boards. Plasterers cut off plaster. Men with muffled barrows carry the residue to the waiting lorries, coming in a dark line up the lane.

In the precious bedroom the real skill is shown. A hand marks out the wall into blocks. A saw with the thinnest of blades cuts the blocks one by one and they are removed onto pallets. Each pallet is wrapped, numbered and carried down the winding stairs. A special lorry, with a heavy tarpaulin, is loaded and checked.

Everywhere dust and debris. Men sweeping, men stepping round men sweeping, glimpses of roof tiles from the inside, and joists exposed to show men working above them.

There is no time for tea, for sitting outside and talking. Though it is noisy, it is also largely silent, with whispered instructions and muttered acknowledgements. Outside the band booms.

Iain is everywhere, encouraging. Susan is everywhere, encouraging. Some of the men she does not even know, but they know her. She is the muse for whom this enchantment is taking place. There has never been a muse so powerful or so fair.

Iain gives the band until midnight, and returns. Its noise is everywhere but Ewan and the Australian are nowhere to be found. Another one, thinks Iain, and Peter will be very disappointed. Iain's wife has finished the washing up and gone home. She knows there is something going on, but she does not care.

He looks into the dining room, but the scene is the same. Time stopped when they drained their glasses and it will not start again until it is ready. Old Donald's moonshine cannot be hastened or hurried. Everyone knows that.

He listens carefully but he can hear nothing except the band. The universe can hear nothing except the band.

Before he leaves he pours innumerable pints of cider. The band does not care that no one is appreciating their talent, because everyone can hear it, including them. He gestures to show that they can help themselves to anything. He mimes his watch, encouraging them to keep going. They are delirious with joy. This is the night of their lives.

It is one a.m. Up at the house there is virtually nothing left inside. The walls are back to stone, with windows framed only by themselves. It is time to start bringing it all down.

A moment of reality. Surely someone should be patrolling the village, watching out for its people, ready to help those who cannot help themselves. Where is the friendly village bobby, or the interfering neighbour who will complain about the noise What about the casual visitor, the driver-through, the tourist who has lost his way Surely not everybody is caught in this night of spells They are. The interfering neighbour At her sister's in Paisley, entwined in the pattern of her old life. She is presently asleep, dreaming of hills and Highlands. When she returns there it will all be the same. Or almost.

The village bobby He was axed, months ago. His station was downsized and shifted, his radio returned and he is working from a police box twenty miles away which only opens twice a week. Thank God for progress!

The tourists, the people who have driven long and hard and are worried that their landlady has gone to bed Iain and Susan have thought of that too. There are men on the only roads in and out of the village, men with cars and breakdowns, and enough theatrical business and busyness to distract a wandering enquirer long enough for something to be done. But there are no wandering enquirers, for this is late at night and the tourist season is regulated by efficient electronics. Thank God for the SVA!

Iain is back at the house. The first difficult part is over and there is time for a brief rest. A bomb, even a smart one, can take a house apart in an instant, but only some very special force, more powerful and infinitely more clever can take a house to pieces in a night and still keep it safe. The walls will come down piece by piece, but first there must be scaffolding.

Nobody ever put scaffolding up quietly, but then nobody ever put scaffolding up to the accompaniment, across acres of moorland and reverberated from ramparts of hills, of the Dark Night Deaths Head Motorcycle Ceilidh Band. It actually seemed louder up here, given shape and substance by being let out into the world to seek and destroy any eardrums which were not in the deepest of hiding.

No neighbours complained because they could not believe it. They thought they were having hallucinations or that the Calor gas boiler was manufacturing perpetual explosions. And some of the closest who might have complained had husbands or sons or fathers who had crept out as the darkness settled and told them to stay inside and do nothing for the whole night long.

The scaffolding is up and Iain tests it. Then, as if being sliced by the blackness of the clouds, the roof loses its slates. Wood is removed from wood, nails from nails. A chimney disappears, stone by stone, and the walls that have held the canopy that protected several generations are lowered in pieces one by one to the ground and carried quietly and unprotesting down the track to be taken away.

Windows come out whole. Harling falls off and is brushed up, sliver by sliver. Light rises in the east and the work continues. After the passage of hours the foundations are reached just at the moment when there is – silence.

Silence after a performance of the – you know their name by now – is breathtaking, or would be if there was any breath left in the world. It is like the creation of a new planet: it is full of awe and hope and wonder. Those birds whose insides had not turned to jelly, tentatively started to sing. But to Iain it spelt only one thing – disaster. There were six lorries in the lane, and – he reckoned – another seven loads after that, including the stuff that had to be brought in. It couldn't be done in silence because if it was, it would be heard.

"Tools down," he said. "Engines off. Have a breather. We have about four hours left before they wake. I need to find out what is happening."

He sprinted down to the hotel, dashed through the kitchen door and met a scene of utter devastation.

The bar was completely denuded of drink. Even the stock of last year's novelty lager which he was hoping to return as it must by now be undrinkable, had gone. There were bottles, cans, crisp packets everywhere. Except on the stage where seven very large, very darkly dressed, very chain-encumbered men were standing in utter stillness.

On the floor in the middle was the bottle of Old Donald's moonshine.

If ever Iain had seen an emergency, then this was it. If there were hours of silence, they would be discovered. Even if they were not, then it would be an added complication to add to those that would coincide with the first waking hours of the Vice Chancellor of Seafield University, the noble lord who chaired the Scottish Visitor Administration, the American multi-millionaire who was the world's soft drinks king, a civil servant who would write everything down and Donald Keays who didn't reckon at present. Their eyes might open not to the world as it must become but to an almost demolished building, and the loudest gothic, hard rock, Scottish traditional band in the business. Standing stock still. Difficult as it would be to make sense of it, some conclusions might easily be drawn, particularly by those who were seeking John Lennon's house on the edge of a small country in Europe.

There was also a journalist – somewhere. Most probably hiding under his bed.

A thought rose to Iain's mind. He grasped for it. There was something about Old Donald's moonshine that he had been told on a night when for fun they had given it to a young man in the bar. It was a rite of passage, though nobody ever got through it unscathed.

Something about the antidote. Something strange that didn't make sense. Something concerning … he had it.

It was said that there was only one thing worse than your first drink of Old Donald's moonshine. It was your second.

It reversed the effect but it left you manic. You couldn't sleep, or eat. It made you give up alcohol altogether after a while, for there wasn't much point, as it left no result and made no difference. It was the end.

Nobody, however, took a second glass voluntarily. You just needed to have it smeared on your lips. It was the absolution of the damned.

Iain had never seen seven people who looked so much like the damned, even allowing for the fact that this was how they wanted to look. He stepped forward and picked up the bottle. They had passed it hand to hand, mouth to mouth (it showed) but fortunately there was a little still left in the bottom. He ran it onto his fingers and with as much tenderness as he could muster in the circumstances and considering the people he ran his finger across each of their lips.

No kiss from a prince to his sleeping beauty ever had such an effect. It was if electrodes had been attached to their skulls. They twitched, and shook, and their eyes popped and then, one by one, they were back and looking round them. They sagged a bit, but Iain pointed to his watch, took his wallet, thumbed through notes, and it worked. The noise came back, suddenly, from nowhere. It was every bit as bad as before, perhaps worse because there had been a respite, and definitely worse because they were now two drams of Old Donald's moonshine further on in their changed lives. He ran from the bar and back up the hill.

"Start!" he shouted, above the din. "Start, because we have got to finish."

They finished. The walls went under the ground and the lorries took the stones away. The soil and grass from the old fank (where nobody went) was brought, and was tipped and poured and straightened. You could faintly see the lines of the turf but a few sheep were brought in and slyly tethered.

Finally they took the fence down and filled in the holes. Then the men stood back and considered a hillside with grazing sheep and an unexpected view that seemed to go on for miles.

There was no longer a house on the hill above the fence. Unless you looked very closely, there never had been.

The men left to sleep. It would be time enough later to consider the miracle they had wrought, if they believed it. Iain took Susan down to the hotel but she was too tired for breakfast. There was also no possibility of eating, given the noise.

He gave her a room key and she went upstairs. He sat in the kitchen and wondered what they had done. The precious debris was safe in an old quarry which he owned and where no one would think to look. He would consider how to re-erect it at a convenient time, though soon, because nothing could remain safely and silently hidden for ever.

He went through to the band and told them to stop. He had almost got used to the sound, and if Susan was sleeping through this, then she could sleep through anything. It took a lot of gesticulating and eventually the pulling of an electric plug. Things did not so much fall quiet as gratefully thank the world for silence.

He helped the band load their van. He gave them their money. They drove off rejoicing that they had had, for once, such a night. Many months later two of them were training to be Presbyterian ministers, one was a revivalist preacher and the rest were settling down to good jobs. They would never know that they were the only living souls known to have tasted Old Donald's moonshine twice. The only living souls known to have been saved by it. Apart from Old Donald, of course.

146

Now Iain had the last task to do. He allowed himself a few minutes dozing, but when the Australian and Ewan surfaced, he told them only that the dining room was not to be disturbed. The guests had taken a drop too much. He would take care of them.

Old Donald's moonshine was almost medically precise in its effect. Who knows what he made it from, but it explained why he lived on his own, almost as far away as it was possible to get. From about the eleven and three-quarters hour, until about the twelve and a quarter after they had put it to their lips, Peter, Charlie, Hiram, Donald and the civil servant woke up, one by one.

Iain was standing by.

He gave them each a large mug of strong black coffee. Then another. When they had recovered speech he told them that it may have been a toxin in the venison. Everyone had been very worried but the doctor (what doctor , moaned Peter) had insisted they were not moved. He had seen it before. And if they slept for a few hours they would feel better.

Hiram was well enough to demand (weakly) compensation. Peter (a hypochondriac) didn't want to die. Charlie thought it was just a hangover and he had had many of those before. The civil servant could not compute. Donald alone knew that whatever had happened, it was not what Iain was telling them.

All of them needed little persuasion to retire for a while to bed, except Hiram who was keen to get the legal processes under way, but couldn't yet make the necessary connection between his brain and his mouth. Donald found himself in a bedroom and using a bed that, he noted as he collapsed onto the quilt, also held Susan. And then Iain asked Ewan and the Australian to stop pawing each other and start tidying the bar. It would take until about Christmas.

147

He rang the suppliers and arranged an urgent delivery of drink, so that he could open that night. There needed to be an air of normality. As he reeled off the list – it was everything – the girl on the phone couldn't believe it.

"By God, you've had some hell of a party there," she joked.

"I tell you," said Iain, "you wouldn't believe it."

And then he too slept.

21. GET BACK

The Vice Chancellor woke without any knowledge of where he was or what he was meant to be doing. It took him several moments to come back to himself and realise what was needed.

If he had been anyone else, or if this were a movie, then you would have heard him yell for Donald, with a sonorous scream that would have reverberated throughout the hotel. But Peter was still – despite everything – made of more dignified stuff. He took time to wash, to change into slightly less casual clothes, and then he went off round the hotel looking for him.

He found Iain in the kitchen, supervising what appeared to be the biggest delivery of drink that anyone could imagine. Iain suggested he waited in the lounge while Donald was located and brought to him. There was still no sign of Charlie or Hiram, though the antiquated switchboard showed that Hiram was now once more clocking up the hotel's profits and the electronic miles. His lawyer's profits were also being massaged.

Iain raised Donald and Susan and brought them down the back stairs to the kitchen. He sent the Australian to serve coffee – Peter was never, even after the night before, averse to beauty. Ewan hovered nearby, for he was developing a terrible case of love.

Susan had been steeling herself to look out of a window, worried that perhaps she had dreamt it all. She walked out of the back door and turned towards the hill.

There was nothing there but a view. Just a few sheep and the landscape beyond.

"So it happened," she said to herself, and bumped backwards into Donald and Iain who had also come out of the kitchen door to stare.

"It happened," said Iain. "Now we must bring it all to a close."

Part III (original and then revised and revised again) of the plan was discussed. To work it needed Donald and Susan to be utterly convincing, and Donald to be utterly mad. It needed Iain to be brought in at the very end, just when things had the potential to go wrong and for him to produce the old photograph and the new one which even now was being carefully prepared by the digital wizard who ran an electronic croft two fields away. It might even need – though they hoped not – a bit of shouting and anger. It certainly held an inevitable P45. Then things could start to get better.

As Susan had no home to go to, she went back up to the bedroom, where some of her clothes had arrived thanks to Calum who had been told to bring them and to say nothing to her except to ask how she was. She changed and went to sit in the bar. She was the only one who felt she needed a drink.

Iain ushered Donald into the lounge, where Peter had got to the stage of stroking the Australian's back while she giggled and asked him to stop. Even that, though, was not enough to divert him from his employee, particularly as he was now in easy reach for shouting.

"What the fuck is going on " he yelled as Donald sat down, the force of the Vice Chancellor's words almost physically jerking him back up, and then back down again.

"What the fuck is going on " he repeated. "Are we in some fucking Brigadoon, where the sensible guys are sent to sleep Where have you been, where is the house, and can we please get the fuck on with it Before I have to die in this God-forsaken place."

The Australian took offence at that, and left.

Donald tried to feign calmness. He did not have to feign fear. He told him that the house belonged to and was lived in by his ex-girlfriend Susan, that he had been protecting her when he said he didn't know where it was, and that last night he had been about to tell them when they seemed to have been poisoned by something. He stressed that he had seen the wall. It was amazing. His ex-girlfriend didn't want them to be told but he knew that they could buy the house because the man who owned it wanted to sell. He thought he could get it for a song. And, finally, he offered to take them to the house, now, this instant. If they wanted.

For a moment Peter thought of going with Donald there and then. Of going without Charlie, of finding a way of delivering it to Hiram for a song plus expenses and by so doing cutting out the oaf who had tried to cut him out. But he also thought that if it was all to be finished, it would be best they were all in it together because that way there would be insurances.

So Charlie was brought down (his hangover was abating, he thought) and told the story. Then Charlie and Peter prised Hiram away from the phone and the six-figure sum in compensation that his lawyer could get if the tests on him could be done that day. All together, with Donald and the civil servant in tow, they walked the long way to the cottage, the long way that Donald said was direct.

The long way had been in the plan, because it was the best for what was to come. First of all you walked beside the sea, and then you turned up the hill, and the house (when it had been there) appeared out of a dip, with the fence below it. But as they approached the dip, Donald seemed to stagger. Peter caught his arm and steadied him.

"What now " he barked tersely.

Donald just stared. He walked back and then forward. He peered around him. He looked at the sky and the sea. He peered back at the horizon. Then, for effect, he gurgled a bit and peered some more.

"What the fuck now " shouted the Vice Chancellor. Charlie had never heard him swear before, and that made him suddenly alert.

Donald kept staring. He looked at the Vice Chancellor and Charlie. He ran towards where the house had been and managed to stutter out three words. He had practised them in his head for all of the previous twenty-four hours.

"It's not there."

There was a long silence. Charlie broke it.

"You must have got the wrong place," he said. "Maybe" – he pointed down the hill – "it's that way."

"No, it was here. Right here. And now it's not. And" – Donald was starting to hyperventilate, though he had not practised that – "And neither is she."

"Calm yourself, man," said Peter.

"What the fuck is going on " said Charlie.

Donald sat down on the verge, quickly, leaving the others standing over him.

"It's not there. It's disappeared."

Peter and Charlie exchanged glances. They were glances that had murder in them but also a touch of fear. Hiram fussed and asked about maps, and references, and suggested that Donald was nuts with tiredness, or that poison, and then felt his own pulse and wondered if this effect would hit him too. The six-figure sum grew in his mind.

Peter and Charlie conferred. Peter then squatted down beside Donald. He pronounced his words very slowly, but with deadly menace.

"Donald, tell us what is going on," ordered Peter. "Tell us right now. WHAT THE FUCK IS GOING ON "

Donald got up and started to wander about the hillside, poking, but not too hard, here and there at bits of grass, with a stick he had picked up. It was the end of a skirting board, the only thing that had eluded them. He strode off along the track, and then back to them. Charlie and the Vice Chancellor looked on. Hiram was still trying to find his pulse.

Eventually Donald came back to them and said, as calmly as he could muster, "I am trying to be calm but I don't know what is going on. The house was here yesterday. I saw it. I was in it and I spoke to her – to Susan. But it is not here now. It has – and it was your words this morning Peter – it has disappeared like something out of *Brigadoon*."

"Fuck *Brigadoon*," said Charlie. "*Brigadoon* is a fucking Yank movie. You are either cheating us, or you are fucking nuts." And then he said, almost as an afterthought, "Either way you're dead."

Unfortunately for them all, Hiram had heard of *Brigadoon*, for he was not a stupid man. He knew that it was a Yank movie but he also knew that it was a movie in which people – people in Scotland – appeared and disappeared. He knew that its sets were wobbly and that people danced, but it was a movie none the less. It didn't lie. It was spooky and he dreaded spooky.

Hiram had not got where he was by being indecisive. He had also not got where he was by showing physical courage. Retreat was urgently called for. Either these guys were up to something or they were all certifiably insane. Perhaps it was that mad cow disease that Phyllis had warned him of. His second wife never wanted to travel to Europe and she was obviously right. It might be contagious. It certainly looked like it was (Charlie and Peter were

153

gawping too now), and it led to piles of burning corpses. Time to scram.

He set off down the hill, his mind already set on phoning a cab and getting the hell out of here as quickly as possible, before the violence started. Or the devil stuff. Or the burning corpses.

He would sue them all if he survived. But first he needed to get away.

Peter and Charlie, suddenly aware of what was happening, scuttled after him, with the civil servant in close pursuit. The civil servant soon returned for Donald, though, and with a firmness that surprised both of them he took his arm and steered him back to the hotel.

Twenty minutes after they had set out, they were sitting again in the lounge, with the door closed and a glass of water in Donald's hands. Hiram was upstairs, packing his case and talking to his lawyer again.

"Now," said Peter. "Tell us exactly what you did, who you saw, and what you think has happened."

Donald went through the same story. The sheep man's letter, the places he had seen ("Skip that fucking rubbish," said Charlie), the decision they had all made, his trip north, his meeting with Susan in the bar, his visit to the house, and then his lies to make some time for both of them, and her precious discovery. The dinner at which he was about to tell them the truth, the blank bit, the walk up the hill and then the fact, the absolute fact, that it had all vanished. He was amazed at his ability to act it out as if he was feeling it all, though only bits of it had happened that way. It was as if he had become, almost for the first time in his life, really alive.

"We need some help with this," said Peter. So Iain was summoned and made sure that he did not come for a good ten minutes, so that Donald could sweat a bit more

154

and Peter and Charlie could contemplate losing what they thought they had.

When Iain arrived he was bland.

"Can I help you gentlemen with something " he asked.

"With quite a lot, I think," said Peter. Peter asked him about the village, about the Lennon story, about whether he knew it and if it was true. Iain confirmed what they had known yesterday. He had lived there, on and off, all his life, he knew the story, but no, he didn't know if it was true.

"Where is the house " asked Peter.

"Well, I shouldn't be saying."

"Look, let me be absolutely straight with you. If the house exists, we will find it. We want to offer money for it. It will be good for everybody here. And I can offer you money too."

Iain played his role to perfection. He agonised for a bit, he looked shifty, he tried to get some money in advance, and then he reluctantly told them that the problem was, well, it was that the house had been, well, demolished, so to speak, some years back it would be. It had stood on the hill, certainly, above the fence, undoubtedly, but that land was just grazing land, nothing special at all now, as the gentlemen could see. The rubble had been used to fill the new pier, and they had needed that, given the weather and the tides, the Lord knows. So if it was true, and of course what he was saying was the gospel truth, then it was no longer true unfortunately for them and for the place, more's the pity.

"But Donald says he was there yesterday. With his girlfriend. And he saw the drawings."

Iain looked knowing. He had heard about things like that. It could be the second sight, but that would be unusual in a Lowlander, would it not, and anyway he didn't believe

155

in such old wives' tales, unlike some, and who is to blame them, for I have heard …

Peter tried to cut him short. But he went on. Might it not be, he had heard, the stress The stress that comes from living in cities and being expected to do too much That and the rock music and drugs. Mental breakdown Early midlife crisis Could it be that Donald had been under pressure recently Was his job at risk, or his personal life They said that rest and recuperation made all the difference but it was hard to see where one would get that, these days, right enough.

Donald just sat, his arms hanging from him like a tired boxer's.

Peter was becoming convinced even though Iain's stage Highlander stuff was grating on his more decisive nature. But was made of less trusting stuff. He didn't understand what was going on, but until he had proof he was not going to give way.

"Show us a picture of the house," he suddenly said. "I think this might all have been a scam, or the work of that bloody nutter," he added, pointing at Donald, "but if there is a picture of the house when it was there, and it isn't there now, then we will know."

Iain protested. He didn't know if he had a picture. Anyway, everyone would tell them the same. And was it not a bit cruel on poor Donald, to put him through any more Particularly as he didn't think there was any Susan either, except a girl of that name who worked in the hotel and was living there, but who was off duty last night.

Peter and Charlie perked up and asked to see her. Iain got up and went for Susan. She played her part too, looking bemused, being asked if she knew Donald, saying that she didn't except that she had seen him that day when he came to the hotel (that was yesterday) and an hour ago when he was walking up the hill with the rest of them. Donald sobbed a bit, but was scared of overdoing it.

Iain eventually got up and went looking for photographs, his reluctance showing from every pore and from all his muscles too. He took a decently long time to come back with a couple of pieces of paper – a dog-eared old picture taken from outside the hotel which showed behind it, up the hill and above a fence, the top storey of what was clearly a house where there wasn't one now. He had found another photo too – one taken last year, he thought. It was a great view of the whole sweep of the village, with the hotel right in the middle and everything covered in snow so that the contrasts were sharp and the light intense. Behind the hotel it was clear that there was only a hill and not even a fence. There were some sheep, though. It was so good it might have been an Allan Wright or Colin Baxter postcard. Which of course it was, though the rest had been removed from sale, at least hereabouts, as the original did not quite match this new version.

Charlie took the pictures outside and examined them in the early evening light. He walked up and down, but pictures didn't lie. There was no house, at least not now. And he couldn't search every inch of the landscape and the inside of every God-forsaken cottage in case they were lying. They were, on balance, probably telling the truth. Donald had clearly lost his mind.

There was a commotion at the door of the hotel, a slamming of doors and then Hiram's taxi passed him, but Hiram did not wave. That avenue was closed too. There would have to be someone else to pay for the next big thing.

So Peter and Charlie admitted defeat. They did not look at each other when they did so, for each was already working out the next move, perhaps against the other. But there was no more to be had here, and certainly no profit and no prestige. This episode was at an end.

The chauffeurs were summoned. They had slept through the night, unconcerned, though a tiny bit of Old Donald's moonshine had been put in their night-time cup of Horlicks in order to help, delivered to their bedroom doors by kindly landladies. They wondered why they felt as if they had a hangover, because both of them were teetotal.

Peter and Charlie agreed to say nothing while they worked out their next steps. The civil servant never said anything, so instead he was told not to write it down. And in case the *Daily Record* man had a photograph his camera was accidentally stolen by Iain as he was waiting to pay his bill, which his paper would not reimburse (though he did not know that yet) as they had just downsized him.

Peter had offered to take Donald with him, to get him sorted out by one of the many psychiatrists or psychologists or therapists whom he knew, or employed, or from whom he could cadge favours. Perhaps there was a new department in all this, he found himself thinking. Stress Management must be profitable.

But Donald didn't want to come and Iain said he would ensure he was looked after that night, that they would call the doctor (and that they would make sure he got to his home, wherever that now turned out to be).

The Jaguars roared into the falling night and Donald – who did feel he was having a breakdown – went back to bed and Susan held him tight and in the middle of the night they made love, sadly and gravely, and then they talked for a little about what future they might make.

Iain stayed behind the bar for most of the evening, allowing Ewan and the Australian to disappear for a time. It was quiet as most of the village was sleeping off the effects of the previous night.

As the hour grew late, and everything was almost silent, two tourists appeared on bicycles, but they had a tent, and all they needed was a visit to the loo and a toasted sandwich, which Iain made for them though the kitchen was closed. It was the least he could do, or perhaps the least he could do to try and feel normal.

He shut the bar on time – a rarity – and when the lights were out he stood at the window by the stairs, looking up the hill to where the sheep could just be seen in the cloudy light, grazing.

He turned to go, and his eyes caught, from the other window, the phosphorescence of the sea and a path of starlight that led away to the horizon. On nights like this, he thought, people believed again in magic. Yet it was all around them, all the time. They just were unable to see.

Perhaps that was just as well. Men and women could have too much magic.

22.. (JUST LIKE) STARTING OVER

A year goes past. Charlie is not allowed to see out his term of office. Fresh thinking being less important than fresh branding, the SVA transforms itself by dropping the pilot and then dropping the name. So C-Caledonia is born. There is meant to be a new strategy too and new promises made to those who have heard it all before but whose capacity for hope remains as strong as ever.

Another year passes. On a slightly misty but very promisingly warm mid-morning of the last Friday of July, the immutable date on which Highland Games are held in this little spot at the very top of Scotland, the C-Caledonia travelling exhibition is being unloaded and set up in the field overlooking the bay, just down from the shop and the petrol pumps.

Susan watches the expensive boards being assembled around the even more expensive caravan. Then the video and computer screens are slotted into place and the loudspeakers start to pump out Celtic rock. She turns back to her own much more modest stall, which consists of an old pasting table, covered by white paper. The threadbare tent in which it sits is one of the all-purpose ex-army cut-down marquees which the Games Committee manages to mend and make do year after year. It smells of old burgers and damp canvas.

"Give me a hand with the stuff from the car," said Donald. "We've only got half an hour before the chieftains' parade comes onto the field, and from then on it will probably be chaos."

"The stuff" is boxes of brochures advertising their business, which was now in its second year. "Highland History" had started out as a way for Donald to try and make or scrape a living. What was more obvious than he put to use his knowledge of the past and his appreciation of the state of tourism by arranging tours for visitors which told the truth about Scotland's past and which utilised only the best facilities

They had expected a slow start, but once the information was on-line enquiries flooded in. Susan was eventually giving a hand in all the spare time she had, but as the new season approached, with heritage tours of every part of the Highlands and Islands sold to an array of overseas and Scottish-based tourists, with tour leaders to brief, with hotels, restaurants, bus and ferry arrangements to make and with Donald scouring the north and west for anyone to help him, it seemed a message from heaven when the SVA transformed itself and in so doing made her redundant. All the tourist offices north of the Highland Line were being closed and replaced by "C-points" as they called them – electronic enquiry machines which would take the place of human beings.

And whilst she settled quickly into the old routine of working with Donald (though now they shared the decision making) the local C-point had not been an unqualified success. Deer gnawed through its telephone line, rodents nibbled its plastic casing, driving rain penetrated its circuit boards and heavy-handed Danes pummelled its touchscreen to destruction. The little enclosure it sat in was a handy place for sheep to sleep and leave their droppings, and to cap it all most people thought it was a cash machine and complained bitterly when it wouldn't give them any money.

But as the tourist office had been sold and was already being converted into a holiday home (the market continued to rise despite a parallel rise in the price of petrol) it was unlikely that the old would be brought back to make up for the deficiencies of the new. Such is progress.

The C-Caledonia exhibition stand at the games was part of the new strategy as well. It demonstrated commitment and allowed visitors and locals alike to find out about other Scottish destinations. It was staffed almost entirely by leggy blondes from Lanarkshire but it was managed by a Latvian. Most of its visitors were kids looking for free pencils.

Donald and Susan arranged their brochures, their panels with large pictures and their free key rings without much hope of significant business. This was a demonstration of presence rather than a sales opportunity, so they both felt quite free to stand outside the tent and watch the procession come up to the field, which marked the start of events.

The chieftain was chosen each year by the Games Committee and nine years out of ten a radio or TV personality or a politician was invited to undertake the role. This year, however, a local person had been selected and Donald and Susan grinned and waved as Iain went past, wearing the chieftain's rosette and carrying a brand new cromag, a badge of office which was presented to each chieftain at the start of their big day. Behind him ambled a gaggle of men and women clad in kilts and assorted other tartanry, and carrying (or leaning on, depending on age) their own special cromags. There was much clicking of cameras and old Lachlan Morrison, thinking that every bit of him looked proudly Highland including his grog-blossom nose, ogled back at the young girls in their shorts.

When it came to time for the opening speech, Iain was brief, entertaining and dignified. Then the real business of the day got under way and within minutes the sound of pipes tuning up was blending with the cheers of the crowd as heavy-set men threw hammers, with the deafening rise and fall of a helicopter engine as it flew brief sightseeing trips to Cape Wrath, with the tapping of dancing feet on the competition stage, with the clink of bottles in the beer tent and in the President's hospitality shed, with the whoops of children on the fairground rides, with the distant rapping of shotguns as they tried to bring down clay pigeons, with the conversations of old friends who met only on this day though they lived within ten miles of each other, with Australian twangs, American drawls, Japanese trills, German grunts and French flourishes, and with the atmosphere of an event which seems ancient even though it has only been running in its present form for a generation or so. Most nineteenth-century Highland Games died away during the First World War and had to be revived, as this one was, in the 1970s. . Even those that take place literally half a world away, like that in Ballarat, have fallen and risen more than once. There, however, Aboriginal race winners are no longer presented with their own full set of Highland dress.

Iain toured every stall, congratulating and smiling, but when he came to Donald and Susan's he gave them a special look. After a brief chat he gestured to them to follow him, and after a few more moments of small talk with the Clan Mackay stalwarts who were recruiting like mad and seemed prepared, like Mormons, to baptise ancestors with the name even if they had no right to it, he drew them off into a quiet corner behind the guy ropes.

"I checked up before I changed into this gear," he said, gesturing to his new kilt. "It should be finished within the hour. It's the best day for it, with everyone down here, and the two men will keep quiet, not least because they did the original removal. When you go back tonight I doubt if even you will notice any discrepancy between the rooms.

163

Ring me when you have seen it to confirm it is all safe and done."

For the first six months they had hardly mentioned the removal of the house. Then they woke up to the continuing dangers, for when broadband arrived in the village Donald (by this time researching his tours) had used Google Earth to get a satellite view of the old township. The pictures on-line being a couple of years old, there bang in the middle was the roof which had been taken down and the fence which no longer existed.

Iain had bought the property and the land on which it sat in such a way as to excite no suspicion from the previous owner. But if he ever returned on holiday or if someone arrived bearing old photographs, or if the civil servant or the journalist ever nostalgically wondered what a satellite picture of the place would look like then there would be problems. A second round of explaining might not be impossible, but it would be harder. Clearly, therefore, it would be best to finish the matter once and for all.

After a lot of deliberation Iain came up with the ideal solution. They would build a new house on the site – a replacement so that those who knew the old one but did not know the secret story would think nothing of the change. It would merely be domestic and architectural progression.

Getting planning permission was as complicated, over-bureaucratic, lengthy and frustrating as ever in rural Scotland, but eventually it happened. Iain undertook the building work, using the men who knew the story and who had been a part of it since the beginning. Certain savings were made because the septic tank and the water supply were already in place, and the foundations were old but strong.

This summer the finishing touches were being put to the inside. Now it was time to place the original wall somewhere within the structure, behind protective lath and plaster, and leave it until they finally decided what, if anything, to do with it.

Donald and Susan were still a little nervous about taking back into their custody the thing that had caused so much trouble, though it had also brought them back together again. But it could not be stored in an old quarry for ever and as their new house was going to be considerably cheaper than it should have been (thanks to Iain) they felt they could not look this particular gift-horse, and their responsibilities, in the mouth.

"Great," said Susan. "And thanks. But you had better get back to glad-handing the visitors and supervising the drams for the regulars."

The summer afternoon passed in a welter of activity. Calum and Mairi came by and chatted, Iain's wife nodded to them across the tent where she was selling home baking on behalf of the SWRI, Ishbel brought them some angel cakes, Donald bought some plants for their new garden and Fergus from the local paper took their picture and wrote down a few words about their business. Then, as they were packing up, they heard a familiar voice boom out across the tent.

"Donald Keays. Still here I see," said the Vice Chancellor. "And is this not the girl who worked in the hotel "

Donald froze as the old world collided with the new, like a meteorite slamming into the earth. But Susan remained the stronger and more flexible of the two, and she was quick to reply.

"It's ... sorry, but I seem to know you. Are you not the man who was here when Donald had his little episode Here with an American and that fat wee man who said he was a lord "

"The very same," said Peter. "I was Donald's Vice Chancellor when he was briefly in an academic career. You are Susan, are you not So the two of you have got together – good of you to look after him."

Donald was still staring at Peter open-mouthed. He gave every impression of being still in the throes of his "little episode" and the Vice Chancellor shot him the standard sympathetic but pitying look he used on all occasions when human feelings were required to be shown.

"Oh, Donald is much better now," asserted Susan whilst trying to kick Donald under the table to stop him gawping. "He is just a bit tired today because we have been here since mid-morning. And what are you doing back in this neck of the woods "

"Business," replied Peter bluntly. "Trying to absorb Jack Ridell's outdoor centre into the university along with his ocean-going training, so that we can keep up our reputation for innovation. I am staying there for a few days and he insisted I came up to the games with him." Then, clearly looking for something to bring Donald into the conversation, he added, "I see someone is building behind the hotel, where you thought you had found some sort of pop music treasure."

Donald still said nothing, and his mouth continued to open and close slowly. The Vice Chancellor began to look a little nervous. The memories were flooding back for him too. So he looked sharply at his watch, then quickly around him.

"Well," he concluded, after that bit of theatrical business, "time's getting on. Nice to see you again, Donald, and of course you, Susan, but I must get back. I need to close the deal tonight."

With this the Vice Chancellor nodded and walked away, keen to put some distance between himself and an ex-member of staff who had, very obviously, not yet recovered from a particularly nasty breakdown. He made a mental note to consult the stress management people again about the case and the prognosis.

Of course it never crossed his mind that something else might be involved, or that there could be a curious aspect to the fact that Donald, in that state, was now clearly partnering a girl whose name was the same as his former girlfriend whom he once claimed had lived in a house with an amazing written-on wall.

The Vice Chancellor had moved on, his relentless search for novelty had fared forward, and the details of what might or might not have been had faded and gone.

"Thank God," exhaled Donald as the Vice Chancellor left the tent and strode across the field towards the car park. "Thank God, but …"

"But nothing," said Susan firmly. "He knows nothing, suspects nothing and is interested in nothing. And like him we need to put it all behind us. So let's finish up here and go for a drink in the hotel." Which is what they did.

Much later they stood in the dusty unfinished lounge of their new house and watched the sun drop towards the sea. On the grey–blue surface of the water a yacht, its yellow sail brilliantly outshining the gathering dusk, slowly moved towards the islands of the north, whose shapes could be dimly glimpsed on the north-eastern horizon. Birds dived in splashes of white round what must be a shoal of fish and above it all a single small orange cloud reflected metallic light back to earth.

They turned and looked again – intently and trying to see some problem – at an expanse of newly plastered wall which ran the length of the room.

After a long pause Susan said, "There is nothing to see. Nothing at all."

They carried on looking. "Nothing," she repeated, moving closer to it. "It really is impossible to tell that there is any small gap behind it, let alone that it hides another wall."

"Nothing," echoed Donald. "Nothing. So it's finished – at least for now."

And with that he took her hand and kissed her on the cheek. Then they both went back to contemplating a perfect summer sunset and a view that would belong to them for ever.